The Magnificent Khan

The Magnificent Khan

A NOVEL *of* LOVE

THERESA McNICHOLAS

AMOURIAM PUBLISHING

THE MAGNIFICENT KHAN

ISBN: 978-0-9852039-2-4

Library of Congress Control Number: 2012903128

Cover and interior design by Symmetry Design

Printed in the United States of America

Dedicated to
All Who Would
Truly Love
& Be Truly Loved

Believe me, if all those endearing young charms,
Which I gaze on so fondly today,
Were to change by tomorrow, and fleet in my arms,
Like fairy-gifts fading away,
Thou wouldst still be adored, as this moment thou art,
Let thy loveliness fade as it will,
And around the dear ruin each wish of my heart,
Would entwine itself verdantly still.

It is not while beauty and youth are thine own,
And thy cheeks unprofaned by a tear,
That the fervor and faith of a soul may be known,
To which time will but make thee more dear:
No, the heart that has truly loved never forgets,
But as truly loves on to the close,
As the sunflower turns on her god when he sets,
The same look which she turned when he rose!

—*Thomas Moore*
Irish Poet & Songwriter

Chapter 1

HONEY COLORED HAIR SOFTLY DRAPED OVER AIMEE's tender features as she knelt with eyes closed and hands together in fervent prayer for the protection of her dear parents. They had flown to France earlier in the day to go to the hospital bedside of Mémé, Aimee's grandmother, her mom's mother.

That morning, grief stricken Pépé, Aimee's grandfather, had called to say that Mémé had gone to the hospital a week earlier with an infection and was now suffering from a severe case of pneumonia. Mémé was not expected to live. Aimee's mother had been very distraught and had to be supported by her father to even get to the car.

Aimee had stayed with her French grandparents a number of times in her short twelve years and had always found them loving and kind. They were good humored and from them Aimee had learned a little French. Aimee prayed for them as well.

In the home of her father's eldest brother, uncle Pierre, and his wife, Lacey, Aimee felt quite alone. Though she knew her aunt and uncle very well, she had never before stayed in their home.

Her aunt and uncle's house was a small place for just the two of them as their children were all grown and had their own families. It was not an area in which the exuberant twelve-year-old Aimee and her lively, rambunctious ten-year-old brother Paul could freely explore and play.

An exhausted young Aimee crawled beneath the covers snuggling deeply to garner warmth against the cold of a winter chill in the air and fell asleep as soon as her head hit the pillow.

Twelve years later, Aimee still remembered in vivid detail what happened next when during the early morning, she was gently awakened to a feeling of great peace and joy.

Aimee thought she must be somewhere between asleep and being fully awake. Gentle spring breezes ruffled the lovely sheer curtains over the partially open windows. Aimee felt comfort in hearing Paul breathing softly in a deep sleep on the narrow trundle bed next to her.

She remembered her wonder at the feeling of serenity in this nether time just before the dawn. Soft light glowed on the eastern horizon. And then, she saw what looked like a person standing near the windows. Surprisingly, Aimee felt calm and inexplicably safe.

His features started to become more distinct, showing the soft face of a gentle looking man. There was a glow to him because she could now clearly see his face, garments and the entire height of him. There were no lights on in the room where she and Paul slept, yet a light seemed to completely illuminate the man as if coming from within.

Aimee raised herself up from the bed to examine him more closely. He was magnificent looking. Aimee had never seen anyone like him before. She thought that if this was a dream she did not want it to end.

He was wearing a long gently flowing white robe with sparkling metallic-like threads of blue, gold and rose pink running merrily through the weave. What looked like a long scarf was wound around his head. Later she would learn it was a turban.

Young Aimee felt there was something splendid about him — the strength of his carriage, the soft glow of his blue eyes flecked with gold, dark golden-brown skin, thick wavy brown hair and a deep smile on his lips. His radiant expression sparkled in his eyes and naturally warmed his entire countenance — as though he smiled a great deal of the time.

She gazed at him in awe. Though Aimee could not remember meeting him before, she sensed they had known each other for a very long time. She also had the distinct impression that he knew a great deal about her. And, she was now certain that this was not a dream.

"Please don't be afraid," he offered. "Be at peace in my presence. I have matters of importance to discuss with you. May I speak with you?" His voice was kind. Aimee could only nod "Yes" as she had not yet found her own voice.

Aimee recognized the feeling of love in the deep, warm eyes of the man who looked at her much like her father often did. She sat up fully and focused her attention on him. She wanted to make sure she carefully listened for every word that he would say.

As the sun was rising, he gently spoke of many things about himself and about Aimee and her family. He told Aimee a few things that he needed her help with, including continuing her prayers for her family.

"Your prayers from last night are being answered."

He continued tenderly, "Your beloved Mémé is preparing to go to heaven soon." Tears started flowing down her cheeks as he paused.

A short time later, Aimee's tears slowed and he continued telling her of many more things, secrets she was not to share until a later time. He asked her to unite with him on his quest for assisting others around the world. Aimee again nodded her little head, affirming her agreement with his request.

After many minutes, he lovingly concluded, "I am your Khan, the noble ruler of your precious heart. Know when you go to sleep at night, you are being transported to my Darjeeling retreat in the majestic Himalayan Mountains.

"Talk with me, tell me any and every thing, and ask anything of me. Call to me whenever you have need of me and know that I am always with you."

And then in a blink, he was gone as if he had never been. Aimee could see that the sun was now fully risen, though it was still a few hours earlier than the time she and Paul usually got up.

She was overcome with gratitude that he would visit and share his heartfelt concerns with her. She cherished the love she felt from him and wanted to contemplate his words.

Aimee laid on her bed for a long time after, softly breathing in the lingering fragrance of aromatic sandalwood and cedar, and recalling his caring looks, words and love. Aimee's young heart soared with happiness and the knowledge that the Khan was like her devoted father — someone who truly loved and cared for her and someone she loved in return. She would do all she could to help him by praying and keeping his secrets for the time being.

Chapter 2

AIMEE SMILED IN MEMORY OF HOW THAT DAY YEARS ago had deeply changed her and how her relationship with the Khan since that time had grown. He came to her regularly during pivotal times in her life.

Like the time he had helped her weather some difficult decisions about who she hung out with in high school. She was starting to be drawn into what was considered the popular crowd, a group of around two dozen people who tended to party regularly and did lots of things together. She liked a number of the people in this group, including a teen boy who was attracted to her. Her regular circle of friends tended to prefer quieter activities.

When she had taken the Khan's suggestion that she might like to check whether or not there were any after school programs she could participate in, she had found an amazing opportunity at a marketing firm to participate in their after school apprenticeship as an office runner and design assistant. When she was approved for the program, she became so busy she simply had no time to go to parties or to go out with the myriad people who asked.

A few months later, some of the partying teens had been drinking and a number of them were seriously injured in a terrible accident, including the boy she had been attracted to. She remembered she had been spared from harm because of her choice in pursuing an idea recommended by Khan.

She realized he had never judged her choice of friends or activities — he had always simply helped her to see what opportunities might be open to her in the moment and allowed her to make her own decisions.

Looking down, Aimee noticed that she held a lovely deep ruby colored peony in her hand. The exquisite beauty and fragrance must have evoked the memory of those suspended-in-time moments that first morning with the Khan. She put the flower aside along with a few others she had gathered to take into her apartment.

Several friends had helped Aimee set up a rooftop garden to grow herbs, vegetables, fruits, flowers, bushes and even a few trees. The apartment complex where Aimee lived was an old refurbished brick building with beautiful original wrought iron.

There was not much open ground in the area so people had been using the rooftops, hauling in rich soil and creating planting beds. Aimee had a small greenhouse alongside her growing spaces so she could keep harvesting through the Colorado winters. The rooftop also provided a night time haven for her to meditate on the vastness of the stars in the Rocky Mountain evening sky.

Aimee went back to happily puttering in the garden, culling the weeds and dead, wilted leaves and old blossoms. The garden seemed to enliven itself with her tender care, like a cat uncurling and purring when softly stroked. She and the garden were both enjoying the crisp autumn morning air and warming sunshine.

"Time to go back to work," Aimee whispered to her invisible garden helpers with a little sigh at having to leave them on such a beautiful day.

As a graphic and web designer, Aimee loved creating pleasing, functional and successful materials and websites for people. The project she was working on was for a sweet woman, Laurie, setting up her online store of homemade essential oil aromatherapy oils, candles, soaps and other gift items. The products were already fast selling and there was a ready market for online sales. The project itself was fun for Aimee. However, what it brought up was Aimee's ongoing desire to create her own business and to work for herself.

Though Aimee loved the company she worked for, especially the people at Signet Marketing, she really wanted to spread her wings. There were clients asking for her specifically and encouraging her to strike out on her own. Laurie had found her through one of Aimee's friends and Aimee was trying to work on Laurie's project on her time away from the office, which was precious little enough as it was.

"I really want to work less — not this grueling eighty to a hundred hours per week. I want to earn great money and enjoy my work and my life. Sounds pretty much like everyone I know.

"Of course, my friends Jeena and Leo have their wonderfully successful boutiques and online store. They keep telling me I played an essential role in helping catapult them to success.

"Maybe they would help me set up my own business. I've got to do something about this dream of mine…" Aimee declared out loud as she absentmindedly raced down the stairs to her apartment, not paying any attention to where she was going.

"Oh…" air whooshed out of Aimee as she had run headlong into something hard and yet simultaneously soft. Unseen hands braced her to keep her from falling. Crushed flowers and loose leaves and petals were strewn over the floor.

"Careful now. Sorry about being in the way." A rich deep baritone voice washed over Aimee as she struggled to stay upright.

"What? Ah… I am so sorry. I wasn't looking and I was talking to myself," Aimee stammered out, straightening herself and looking into the depths of the sparkling eyes of a most handsome stranger. His look was of welcome surprise at the awkward situation of Aimee being in his supportive embrace.

"I heard you talking and I was also distracted listening to your conversation, rather than noticing you were coming around the bend at the same time I was standing here ready to exit to my floor." His low voice resonated with an echo in the stairwell. "Is this also your floor?"

For a few moments Aimee was speechless, staring at the strong chiseled lines of this man's cheekbones and clean shaven face. His golden skin was darkly tanned. Dark, thick, wavy hair hung below the top of his shirt collar. Long, dark, thick lashes — Aimee thought, "seems too lovely to be wasted on a man"— framed soft brown eyes which at the moment had a glint of humor in them.

"Wow! Double wow!" popped out of Aimee's mouth uncontrollably. Quickly she recovered enough to stutter, "I mean… oh dear… okay, embarrassing moment… I'm an artist, a designer actually and you look so incredibly well put together." By this time Aimee had flushed a deep shade of red-pink. She could feel her cheeks burning.

With a good hearted chuckle, the stranger let Aimee go. Laughter twinkled in his gentle eyes as he extended his hand in greeting, "So I've been told. My name is Gavin. I'm very happy to meet you."

"I'm Aimee. And, again, I'm sorry to have run into you like that."

"No harm done. Just your flowers are a bit crushed here," Gavin responded as he picked up petals and stems from the floor. "I'm going to visit my grandaunt on this floor in number three. Are you heading in?"

"Oh, yes," said Aimee as she berated herself for not being able to control her thoughts or her speech around this man.

She observed that he was impeccably dressed in very expensive clothes and shoes, which was unusual attire for anyone frequenting these modestly priced apartment complexes. She did not know that he frequented this building often to see his grandaunt. Aimee realized that she had yet to really thank him. "Umm… I'm in apartment number five if I can offer you coffee or tea for saving me from tumbling."

"Not today as I am having tea with my grandaunt. Could I take a rain check?"

"Yes, of course," Aimee mumbled aloud.

When Aimee closed the door to her apartment behind her, she let out a deep breath. Her heart was pounding. A headache was starting at her temples. She looked down to see her dirt covered clothing and hands and arms. Aimee was sure her face must also have dirt on it. Worst of all she had worn her dumpy, stained grey sweats to work in the garden and even had some dead leaves in her ponytail.

"And," she thought, "how could I have invited that elegant, impeccably dressed man to have coffee or tea with me looking like this?"

Aimee continued to chide herself, "Good grief, Aimee, how stupid of you inviting this stranger to your place. Of course, he's not interested and not available. He's going to see the wonderful old lady in three. What has gotten into you? So what if he's tall, dark and handsome. This is crazy! Besides, there's dear Chad. What's wrong with me? This is too much to think about. Just go get cleaned up and get to work."

Chapter 3

GAVIN STOOD AT GRANDAUNT BERTIE'S DOOR patting dirt off his suit jacket and hands and calming his racing pulse. He had been startled by his instant attraction to the enchanting, dirt covered, garden-fairy like woman. Who was this tongue-tied Aimee?

He laughed remembering her surprise and that she let slip an unbridled and enthusiastic, "Wow!" when examining him. He had spoken truthfully when he said he had often been told about his good looks — though he couldn't remember it ever being proclaimed so innocently and so spontaneously before.

With these thoughts came a smile as Gavin knocked, opened the door and entered Bertie's cozy and light filled apartment. His white haired grandaunt with arms outstretched hurried over to greet him with her usual warm hug filled with love. Whenever he was in the city, he came to see her. Bertie had always been an inspiration to him growing up and he cherished his time with her.

He noticed appreciatively how the dining room table was

set with her favorite fine china that she had brought with her from England in her twenties. Bertie had made fresh baked scones, finger sandwiches and English tea. Though this full English tea service was usually enjoyed in the afternoon, she served it mid-morning to accommodate when Gavin could come to visit her.

Bertie's apartment was comfortably decorated and furniture well worn from many years of use. She sat Gavin next to her on a heavily cushioned bench at the dining table so they could sit side by side, and she could rest her hand upon his arm and enjoy the warmth of the feel of him while he ate.

They talked easily and freely as only those who have known and loved each other for a lifetime can do. When the conversation turned to what had happened in the stairwell and to Gavin asking about Aimee, his grandaunt cocked her eyebrows and there was a noticeable gleam in her eyes.

"Ah yes, my exuberant neighbor next door, Aimee Beaumont. I've gotten to know her this past year. She's a graphic artist and web designer. Lovely girl. She created and tends the gardens on the rooftop. She has taken me up to see them. They are truly wonderful, and there is a spectacular view of the city."

Gavin's good looking face showed his confusion. "Grantie, there is something about my reaction to her that has me puzzled. Never have I felt so electrified or attracted to someone so instantly, especially when they are covered with dirt and debris. You know I have met hundreds of beautiful and interesting women. Yet this woman who looked almost more like a lovely fairy than a woman has me…enthralled."

"Darling, maybe you can find out more about her by offering to assist her. Aimee has told me a number of times that she wants to start her own business. You've started so many new businesses and ventures over the years, and I've watched you grow them into gigantic successes around the world. You could advise her about what to do. You know you are amazingly successful and a brilliant business strategist.

"She currently works for Signet Marketing in downtown Denver, not far from here. She is one of their top designers. As I've been saying, maybe you can help her and get to know her in the process. If I were you, I'd go over to her place right this moment. Her apartment is as interesting as she is. And, at least you can get her phone number."

Gavin sighed, "Grantie, I love you so. What would I ever do without you. I can handle multi-million dollar business decisions in a blink of an eye. Yet, unlike around most other women, when it comes to this Aimee, it seems I cannot even think straight."

Bertie laughed wholeheartedly, "Gavin, I love you so. I'm sure you'll figure yourself out. Thank you for coming to visit me today. I always enjoy our time together."

Chapter 4

AIMEE HAD BEEN CONCENTRATING SO DEEPLY ON setting up her client Laurie's online store that she did not hear a knock. Instead, she heard a deep voice calling her name in a way that sent a shiver up her spine. He even used a soft French accent like her mother used for her name.

"Ai-mée, are you here?"

"Yes, I'm sorry I didn't hear a knock. Come on in. I'll be right there." Aimee shouted as she quickly saved her files and went into the living room.

She found Gavin looking intently at her large poster sized photo art — unique composite pieces using her own photographs and available images of the Universe from Hubble telescope and microscopic lab images from various sources.

The large windows and high ceilings in a spacious open floor plan provided an abundance of natural light and a sense of airy lightness throughout the living room, dining area, and kitchen. An eclectic blend of furnishings and décor gave an impression of chic style. The art was vibrant and rich. Aimee had designed and created this area, and all of her apartment, to be inspiring, energetic and welcoming.

Turning to face Aimee, Gavin's smile dazzled her and further lit up the already bright room, "I came to bother you enough to ask for your phone number so that I might take you up on that rain check."

"Hmm, I see. By the way, how was your visit with Bertie?" Aimee asked, avoiding his request for her telephone number.

"I cherish each and every visit with Bertie. She is my dearly beloved grandaunt, my mother's sister, and a second mother to me.

"Bertie told me you have befriended her. Thank you for doing so. I try and visit her at least once a week whenever possible. With only me living in the Denver area now, she doesn't get as many visitors as when my parents, sisters and brother were all living here." Pointing toward Aimee's wall, Gavin asked, "Do you also sell your art anywhere? These are incredible pieces."

Aimee hesitated for a moment, "No, I have only made individual pieces for myself and family and friends. To me, I consider them personal love notes to the person who is to have one. Would you like one? Oh dear, I mean I need to get to know someone before I can create one for them…"

With a wide grin, Gavin continued, "So, we would have to get to know each other first, and then you could create my unique love note piece of art?"

Aimee felt her cheeks uncharacteristically redden for the second time around this man. "Yes, I guess that's true."

Stammering she added, "Though I don't think we will be

getting to know each other that well, at least in any personal way, not any time soon." Then, Aimee whispered so quietly so that Gavin would not hear, her final words to herself, "If ever at all."

Even freshly washed without makeup, her long golden brown hair pulled back into a ponytail, and in plain black and grey pants and top, Gavin thought she was absolutely lovely. Her striking features and tanned glow seemed to demand beautiful color in her clothing palette, though he would not tell her until he knew her better. Blushing as she was now just seemed to heighten his attraction to her. Gavin was used to blatant flirtation, and he was discovering Aimee was an innocent, unused to seduction or intrigue.

Gavin wanted to stop causing her feelings of embarrassment, yet he could not help enjoying their authentic conversation. He realized with surprise that Aimee was unwittingly winning more of his heart the more he was around her.

"Would you have time and be willing to show me your apartment right now? Bertie likes your place and thought I might like to see it." Gavin asked softly, more to rouse her from her uncomfortable silence than needing to converse. He found himself wanting to stay longer.

"What? Oh, yes, um, ... I guess that's fine. I've just managed to clean up after myself." Aimee was feeling that yet again she had made a blunder in giving out too much personal information. He seemed a little too charming. Aimee's thoughts roamed to wonder, "Was he some kind of shallow charmer and seducer of women?"

While staying seated a little longer, Aimee swept her arm

around the large open room and said, "As you see this is my 'great' room of living room, dining room and kitchen. The design is to invite a sense of being alive and of comfort and welcome. Let's go down the hall and I'll show you the rest."

Aimee rose a little unsteady on her feet. Gavin kindly stepped near her and grabbed her arm to keep her standing. "It seems I am here to help keep you steady today."

"No," Aimee thought, "you are the reason for my unsteadiness today." At least she had not said this aloud so he could hear.

Gavin was thoroughly impressed with Aimee and her apartment. Everything was neat and seemed to be designed to elicit an overall cozy cheerfulness. Her office and accompanying bathroom were modern and sleek yet done in colors and small décor elements to keep it feeling energetic, creative and comfortable. Gavin observed that Aimee had strategically placed colorful groupings of candles that perfumed the air with the sweet smell of beeswax and mood elevating aromatherapy.

Aimee's bedroom was a sanctuary — different yet complimentary to the rest of her home, it was filled with an exotic blend of scents, sights, and textures of designs and fabrics of the Orient and the Middle East — all he might imagine for her, with his well trained and intuitive talent for the look and feel of these particular styles. With a knowledgeable expertise, Gavin recognized that Aimee was truly gifted in design and thought that it looked like she just needed a little assistance with her personal appearance.

That night Aimee lay in bed breathing deeply of the gentle

sandalwood and jasmine fragrances wafting through her room. She was contemplating what had happened today with the amiable stranger. Gavin had mentioned visiting the rooftop garden when he came next time.....next time. Before she could complete her thoughts, Aimee had fallen fast asleep.

Chapter 5

"Hooray! A strike! Beat that Gav..." Hawk was whooping it up as he had made the first strike of their animated bowling game. Hawk, John, Connor, Ahmed and Gavin were having this week's meeting at the bowling alley.

These five outstanding young men had met and become the best of friends eight years ago in their freshman year of college. All of them had favored studying business and international trade. These creative, innovative, athletic, and good-natured young men had been quickly magnetized to each other.

Ideas sparked among them and less than a year later they launched their first, of many to come, businesses under the umbrella of Holbrook Enterprises, Inc. At the time, Gavin contributed the majority of the original financial assets into the company based on his earnings from a small gadget he had invented earlier so the other men thought using his surname, Holbrook, honored that. Also, they all liked the ring of distinction in the name.

Their businesses now spanned the globe, had interconnecting boards of directors, and were rooted in a wide variety of industries and activities, including technology, software, fashion, cloth making, weaving, sustainable community services, and biochemical and biophysical research, with fingers in myriad other enterprises. Some of the companies had patents in their unique areas of expertise.

These young entrepreneurs had discovered that they were much more productive and creative in their meetings when they actively engaged in doing something. They were all athletically built and tall, ranging from five-eleven for Ahmed to six-four for Hawk, and had lots of energy and boisterous spirit.

With kinesthetic learning and communication styles common to the five of them, doing sports and physical activities during their meetings seemed all important to their sanity and kept them united and focused on the issues at hand.

They had long ago set up meetings while hiking, biking, skiing, sailing, and various other activities to keep their hearts pumping and their spirits elevated, and to be more relaxed and inspired while they dealt with business matters. They also created games and picnic events of rugby, cricket, softball, flag football, and other matches that suited a specific company's staff and their families.

This turned out to be a fantastic way to team build and encourage good-natured sportsmanship with company leaders and employees around the world. They had found it an effective way to create sincerely open dialog. Many fruitful ideas had emerged during these gatherings.

In between throws of bowling balls down the lane, they

threw ideas and decisions back and forth among them. And, whoever happened to be sitting, waiting for their turn became a moderator of sorts and, as desired, note taker into their digital notebook or whatever mobile device was most convenient at the moment. Though they did not need the notes, they all loved using their various gadgets, trying new ways to work with them and thinking up other helpful gizmos and applications they might consider inventing.

Their current agenda included discussions on hiring a company to create advertising and an online presence for one of their new ventures that included the recent acquisition of a fledgling fashion house and clothing distribution company.

During these discussions, an image of Aimee appeared in the forefront of Gavin's mind. Thoughts of Aimee came up frequently in the few days since meeting her. He recalled she worked as a graphic and web designer and remembered how much he had been impressed with her artistic talent.

He tried to recollect the company she worked for. "Do any of you remember working with a marketing company in town? Or with a graphic designer named Aimee Beaumont?"

"Seems familiar. Let me ask Bonnie. She's such a whiz at keeping track of who we've done work with. I'll send her a text message right now, and we can see what she comes up with." Connor commented thoughtfully as he began to tap out the message on his cell phone.

"Connor, your bowl." Ahmed sounded from the lane after he had scored a spare.

After several game rounds, they decided it was time to get some dinner and finish up their meeting. They went to a popular nearby deli. They sat at a booth toward the back, ate thick juicy sandwiches, and reviewed their mental and digital notes, highlighted points of interest and finalized their decisions and action items.

Connor spoke up part way through chewing on a bite of his flavor packed pastrami sandwich, "Hey, Bonnie's just texting saying she has quite a bit of information for us on our request. Want me just to get her on the phone so she can tell all of us at once?"

"Yeah, that'd be great," Gavin was quick to reply.

"Hey Bonnie, we've got you on speaker and we're in the back at the deli so we should hear you fine."

"Hi all. Well, the company we worked with was Signet Marketing in downtown. It's a medium sized company that has done a little work with us at headquarters here and a couple of jobs with one of our clothing branches in Los Angeles. Aimee Beaumont is one of their top designers. She was the primary one working with the LA office to create some promo pieces for them.

"What they said was that the pièce de résistance was a collection of small fashion models, designed almost like paper dolls, artfully displaying some of their new clothing designs. Accompanying these were adjustable self-adhesive stickers of accessories that could be moved from model to model. Our people and their buyers and clients absolutely loved them. They have been so effective in increasing sales that they've had several additional print runs.

"The staff expressed top rated satisfaction with Signet. However, their glowing praise highlighted Aimee as the star. It seems the staff liked her professional collaborative way of working with them and her fresh, creative ideas, foremost being those cutouts I just mentioned. That's pretty much it."

Gavin thanked Bonnie and turned off Connor's phone.

John perked up, "What about this Aimee person? Do any of us know her?"

Gavin pondered John's questions about Aimee and thoughtfully responded, "I believe she could be someone who can help us develop the marketing materials and the website for our newly acquired fashion house as well as other company graphic and web design projects. I admired some of Aimee's work when I ran into her recently."

Though these were all truthful statements, Gavin had not wanted to reveal the whole story of his literal run in with Aimee, knowing his friends would find ways to tease him and want to know more personal information about her. At least for now, he wanted to closely guard how her eyes, with their delicate shape, hazel sparkle and wistful glimmer had deeply affected him and how they continued to come into his mind, like a dream.

Gavin continued, "Aimee mentioned she is trying to set up her own company and maybe we can become her primary client. Or maybe, we can have Signet Marketing handle some of our projects and Aimee on her own can handle others. I guess this is something we can look into.

"Connor, you on board with checking this out? Of course, you and Ahmed have the India trip planning. Hawk, you're handling the new acquisitions transitions. And, John, you've got all the financial navigating with the newest corporate tax filing guidelines. I have our new research and development projects going. What do you guys think?"

"Sounds great to me," was echoed by the others.

Connor added, "Gav, I'll check out the Aimee Beaumont situation and create some ideas we can consider in the next couple of days. Ahmed and I already have much of the planning done for the India trip. Reminder to all that Gav, Ahmed, Ayesha and I are scheduled to leave for India in six weeks."

This upcoming trip to India had been extended to a four-month stay to afford them the needed time to visit a number of their numerous facilities there, meet with company staff and various business associates, engage in some vital research and brain- storming with partners, and attend the wedding of two friends in New Delhi.

Connor contemplated how he and Gavin, the bachelors of the group, tended to be the most practical choices for these extended international trips. It helped that he and Gavin enjoyed being steeped in the cultures of where they traveled and spending time with their many friends and associates around the world. India happened to be a big favorite with both of them so they were looking forward to this trip.

The married men of their group generally liked to stay close to home. The wives were regularly consulted about the plans and activities of their husbands, especially relating to long trips abroad, such as this one coming up.

Along with their wives, Hawk and John had elected to stay home this time. Hawk wanted to stay near his gentle Norwegian wife who recently discovered she was eight weeks pregnant with twins and would not be traveling anywhere for quite some time to come.

John's gracious Asian wife was a stay-at-home mom caring for two small children, and John liked to spend as much time with his family as possible. These two would remain home and carry on business at their Denver headquarters.

Ahmed and his wife, Ayesha, were both from India and had jumped at the chance to take this trip. Ayesha had many relatives and friends who she planned to visit while Ahmed conducted business.

These husbands had often remarked that their wives were equal partners in many of their decisions regarding company matters. Gavin had always encouraged the inclusion of women to provide a feminine perspective and these astute three were vital assets.

Connor concluded, "All of us going on the India trip are scheduled to meet together and review the details of our itinerary next Friday."

Gavin and Ahmed nodded in acknowledgment. They departed the deli satisfied with their meal and the results of their meeting.

Chapter 6

AFTER AN INTENSE WEEK OF WORK AND A DIFFICULT and emotional dinner date with her boyfriend Chad, Aimee had gone home, vegetated in front of the television and somehow had dragged herself to bed, falling instantly and deeply asleep. During the night, she felt…

Warmth… What a wonderful feeling to be warm… and to feel …

Aimee looked up and found she stood in the long familiar grand entryway of a large cavernous room, resplendent with elegance and the brightness of glowing light. An unbelievably soft and luxurious white carpet covered the entire floor.

Across the room were windows that rose from the carpeted floor reaching up to the two-floors-high ceiling. Crystal clear glass framed the spectacular view of snow capped mountain vistas of the majestic Himalayan range.

Nearby, tall, grand sentinels of Himalayan white and blue pine, deodar, and spruce trees stood. Gorgeous rhododendron blossom laden bushes gave breathtaking dimension and depth to the view.

A tall and broad shouldered man stood facing the enormous glistening marble fireplace with strong, powerful hands clasped behind his back.

His shoulder length brown hair was highlighted with streaks of gold and red from the fire. He radiated an aura of extraordinary majesty.

An iridescent, electric blue linen garment draped elegantly over his finely tailored loose fitting tunic and pants. His comfortable, yet royal looking attire and bearing augmented his magnificent grandeur.

When he turned toward Aimee, his entire face was lit up with an incredible smile and his twinkling eyes overflowed with a deep love that radiated like lightning throughout his entire being and engulfed Aimee clear across the room.

"Khan!" Aimee exclaimed with pure delight.

On winged bare feet Aimee ran to him over the carpet, which felt like soft, fluffy clouds. He opened his long and powerful arms in a warm and welcoming embrace. Aimee was enfolded in brilliant blue linen cloth that emitted little sparkles of light and an aromatic sandalwood scent that wafted sweetly around her.

Aimee felt the soft, fine weave of his tunic. All of her senses were heightened as she, with her whole heart and soul, cherished this moment with him.

Aimee's entire body burned with what she saw as a concentrated deep pink energy field. She felt like her physical heart was expanding to contain this familiar energy of what she knew to be mystical love flowing between Khan and her.

When she reluctantly stepped out of his embrace, Aimee brushed against an enormous bouquet of brilliantly colored flowers in a transparent blue crystal vase. The floral perfume was exquisite. She comfortably plopped herself near the fire on the lush carpet close to his finely carved chair.

Khan, with his usual natural regal grace, sat and turned to Aimee, "Dear daughter, come, tell me what's on your heart." Aimee always told him about what was going on in her life whenever she came to see him here at his Himalayan retreat dwelling. Aimee started to tell him a few things about what she was feeling and circumstances in her life. He listened open-heartedly to what she was telling him and was starting to say …

Bzzzzz… "Oh no, not yet," Aimee moaned. She warily opened her sleep heavy eyes and slapped off the annoying alarm. She wanted so much to continue with him. Instead, she was slowly awakening to a new sunrise and back to her solitary single life in her apartment in the busy city.

As Aimee took a few moments to meditate upon her time with the Khan, she realized that she felt an intense burning in her chest. She saw varying shades of brilliant ruby red and pink fire fully engulfing her physical heart and lungs.

In her mind's eye she could also see Bernini's famous sculpture, the *Ecstasy of Saint Teresa*, that she had studied about in an art class. She remembered that Bernini was inspired by the mystical ecstasy of Teresa of Avila being consumed by the great love of God. She realized that Khan had impressed a gift of some extra love into her today.

Aimee closed her eyes again and tried to get back to Khan.

No such luck. It was time to rise and shine and get on with her fully scheduled day.

Aimee noticed a sound of whispered voices and went into her living room. Her television was on with Giada explaining how to prepare some delectable Italian dish. Then, with a jolt, she was reminded of last night. She had spent hours mindlessly watching a dizzying array of shows as she tried to get over being dumped by her boyfriend of almost two years.

Well, she had not exactly been dumped. Chad wanted to still be friends, and, of course, they were friends, the best of friends and had been since they were teasing each other in second grade. Of course, that had been the problem all along — they were just simply friends without the romantic all-consuming passion of lovers.

Chad had said, "Aimee, you know we are not in love with each other. We care deeply for each other as a brother and sister might."

Certainly, they had kissed and hugged. Neither of them had wanted to go any further, and last night he was expressing what both of them already knew.

Chad was a vitally handsome and popular man. Two of Aimee's married friends, Jeena and Alkisha, had paired them up and considered him a grand "catch." Chad had been her constant companion at the events of her friends and family. Even Aimee's younger brother, Paul, really thought Chad was "cool."

So now she was alone again as she had been before having exclusive dates and time with Chad. Of course, she had her best girl friends who did lots of things together. However, most of them now had husbands or longtime male partners who often joined them. And Chad would continue to share in their activities as well. He and Aimee just would not be an exclusive couple.

After flicking off the television, Aimee wearily headed to the shower thinking, "I really wonder what's wrong with me. No excitement. No passionate love affairs. Haven't even ever had any truly serious, heading-toward-marriage relationships. And then I act and react stupidly around a complete stranger who I only know by his first name, Gavin." With a deep sigh, Aimee readied herself for a busy day.

Chapter 7

RIGHT ON TIME, AIMEE ARRIVED TO WORK AT THE modern office building in downtown Denver and found her boss, Ivan Polovtsev, of Signet Marketing waiting impatiently for her.

Aimee loved her job in this mid-sized marketing and design firm. She had worked hard through taking classes at the local colleges and teaching herself graphic design while enduring a low paying job, living in a cramped apartment and often resorting to ramen noodles and mac and cheese out of a box to become what she was today — a talented and award winning graphic designer.

Ideas seemed to somehow bubble through her, and Ivan and their clients sought her out for those solutions perfectly suited to their needs. Aimee's love of design brought together her innate sensitivities to color and her special understanding of the essence behind those colors and visual and graphic elements.

Her perceptive appreciation of natural beauty and keen insights into design gave her work a special quality that few in the industry could emulate. Fortunately for her, Signet Marketing had recognized her potential in her earliest beginnings by hiring her on as an office runner and design apprentice — the opportunity Khan had brought to her attention when she was a teenager.

Today, Ivan was unusually impatient and had immediately accosted her, wanting to know the status of all her projects. Aimee looked quizzically at Ivan.

"Now?" she asked even though she already knew the answer.

"Yes, within ten minutes in my office. Bring the spreadsheets of all your projects and their status. Be thorough."

Aimee winced at his uncharacteristic briskness. She also noticed he was frowning fiercely.

She raced to her office, switched on her computer, added a few updates to her projects list, and printed out the documents. She hastily grabbed the sheets of paper and ran to his office. She breathlessly thought, "Whew, eight minutes."

Ivan gave Aimee a quick glance as she handed him his copy and sat across from him. His frown and apparent agitation made her nervous, and she was never nervous around her usually kind and calm boss.

"Well?" Ivan barked. A startled Aimee jumped at his curt tone and straight away went into her review of the projects on her list with him in minute detail, considerately answering his probing questions.

With guileless hazel eyes staring straight at Ivan, Aimee shored up her courage and voiced her puzzlement, "How unusual. Ivan, you have always trusted me with the details on my projects and never asked so many in-depth questions."

With a shrug and huff, Ivan blurted, "Can you take on some new assignments exclusively? Doing all of the managing and idea generating yourself? Of course, you can get some assistance from the team."

"Oh… Well… Let's see. If you can wait for me to tie up a few loose ends, I can finish up the most critical jobs I have.

"I would like to complete the mock-ups on the Waverly job and create the final layouts for four other projects. I believe the rest of what I have could be passed to the rest of the team. What exactly do you have in mind?"

Aimee felt a small flutter in her stomach in anticipation of what she considered to be a little excitement and simultaneous dread and fear at what might be coming her way.

Ivan begrudgingly agreed and added, "Clear your desk of all projects by Thursday of next week."

Aimee wondered to herself, "What! That's only seven days, including Saturday and Sunday, my days off. Almost impossible and why?"

"Ivan, what's going on? Do you have some secret assignment or what?" Aimee asked with a feigned lightness.

"I'm worried whether we can handle everything coming our way. We have a couple of big new jobs that Jane and Roger have just been assigned. These clients have requested a quick turnaround and will tie up most of the marketing, video and design teams.

"Most importantly, we have a special new client who specifically requested you work exclusively on all their projects with them. They own a phenomenally successful, high profile global company."

Aimee was amazed to know that her work was being requested by such a client. Happy over this recognition of her creative abilities, she no longer fussed over what she had to get done within such a short time.

In the meantime, Ivan had apologized for letting his feelings of overwhelming tension spill onto her. "I'm sorry for my rude behavior earlier. It's like the saying goes, when it rains, it pours, and I don't seem to be handling this downpour very well. Thank you for meeting the challenge and being willing to help with all this."

The rest of the week and weekend was a whirlwind of activity as Aimee had to accomplish what seemed the impossible — finishing or delegating the thirty plus projects she had going.

Chapter 8

On Sunday, during the frantic weekend of Aimee's work, her brother, Paul, was celebrating his birthday which Aimee absolutely wanted to attend. She could hardly believe that her little brother was turning twenty-two. She loved him so very much. They had shared a great bond while growing up that was still maintained now that they were both adults.

The party was a large scale barbeque planned for him at one of his friend's houses. Aimee had forgotten that Chad would be there until she ran right into him, quite literally, with the food on her plate flying over the side. Fortunately, the succulent, boneless chicken smothered in barbeque sauce, potato salad, and other food had not landed on either of them. All of it had just plunked onto the grass. An awkward moment ensued where they talked to each other politely as Aimee felt a mixture of warmth and sadness.

Almost immediately, two golden retrievers bumped both Chad and Aimee out of the way to get at the spilled food. In a flash every last bit of food had been gobbled up leaving the grassy area licked clean.

"Ah, Duke and Duchess, have you been on the lookout for food?" Aimee laughingly observed.

Chad good-naturedly joined in as they both gave Aimee's longtime family pets a good rub down. With Aimee and Paul both out of the house, Duke and Duchess were currently keeping her dog-doting parents company. Chad had been to Aimee's family home often enough that the dogs considered him part of their family circle, and they now happily licked both Aimee and Chad.

With the ice broken, Aimee then felt free to chat amicably with Chad. They caught each other up on a few things and even shared a warm hug in parting, as they had regularly done for many years. Duke and Duchess followed Chad as he walked away.

Katy, one of Aimee's dearest friends, was instantly at Aimee's side. She had seen Aimee and Chad's encounter and noticed how unusually stilted they were when they had first seen each other. Aimee suddenly remembered that in the rush of everything no one knew of Chad and her resolve to be friends instead of a couple.

Aimee grabbed Katy's arm and asked her to please find Jeena, Alkisha, Hope, Gabriella, and Liza. Aimee decided it was much better to tell all her friends at once. As they gathered and Aimee got a new plate of food, Aimee noticed Chad over talking with her parents. "Oh well, he might be telling them the news," flitted through Aimee's thoughts.

The "girls" as they called themselves had long ago become women. What an awesome group they were. Uniquely different in looks, backgrounds, faiths, and professions, every one of these women was stunning in their own unique way. Each woman's loveliness came from a wholesome and radiant well-being — the natural glow that emanates from people who care for their own mental, emotional, spiritual and physical health, as well as that of others around them.

Their attractive, well toned bodies were a living testament that none of them ascribed to the skinny model type body. They kept fit by simply enjoying life and engaging in health sustaining lifestyles — getting out in nature, walking, exercising, eating well and with pleasure, practicing various forms of yoga, qigong, or meditation. They liked to say they knew how to "work hard, pray hard and play hard."

These women shared intelligence, talent, grace and integrity. They were well respected in their own chosen professions. A few started life in poverty and a few in bounteous wealth. Now, every one of them had their own financial independence.

They had met at a summer camp during high school where they worked mentoring kids as camp counselors. Learning outdoor skills, riding horses and caring for lots of freedom-seeking kids, including a few hellions, together they had cemented their friendship into a deeply bonded, abiding sisterhood.

Now they gathered around Aimee as she related the details of Chad wanting to just be friends. Aimee also shared a little of her news about work. The girls' reactions about Chad varied from amazement to prescient knowing.

Liza expressed it best, "You're giving up Chad? He's just such a wonderful guy. Though I suppose all along, you two have seemed more like brother and sister rather than lovers. Will you be okay especially when he and you are both around, like…at this party?"

"Yes, actually Duke and Duchess helped today." Aimee answered realizing that she probably would be okay as long as Chad and she could still be friends. Chad had been her friend for so long that her heart ached to think they would no longer be close.

When some of the girls were departing, Aimee's parents, Pierre and Claire Beaumont, came over to share warm hugs. The three of them wore loving looks as they chatted pleasantly and got caught up on each other's latest news. Because Aimee had been so busy, she hadn't talked with them in a couple of weeks. Usually they talked every few days and got together every week for lunch or dinner.

She realized how much she had missed seeing them over these last few weeks. She could have used the comfort that she was now experiencing from them. Her parents had expressed their concern for her when she announced the news about her and Chad's breakup and were encouraged to know that Aimee and he would continue to stay friends.

Aimee's mother held her in a tight and loving embrace as Aimee shed a few brief tears over the situation. After more supportive hugs with both her mom and her dad, she and her parents parted with a promise to get together for dinner soon.

Chapter 9

By late Tuesday, Aimee found that all her projects were completed or had somehow magically been handled. She could not trace the details of how it had all happened. She had delegated some of the work that needed to carry on and had finished the details she had to complete herself.

Now, relaxing on her couch, she was suddenly hit with panic as to what to do about preparing herself for the meeting with the Holbrook execs on Thursday. They were to begin in the morning at eleven in the office conference room. At noon a specially catered lunch would be served in the dining area. The meeting would continue more casually through lunch. After lunch, everyone would reconvene in the conference room to finish up. Overall, there would be almost four hours of discussion and collaboration.

What her boss, Ivan, had told her was that in addition to himself, key company staff, Kristie, Tenzing, Robby, and Aislinn would be in attendance, with Aimee in the lead. Usually, it was the other way around where one of the others was in the lead, and she was just there as a team participant.

Now that she was liberated from the intense focus on her work, Ivan's causal comments about the importance of looking her professional best for the new client was penetrating her weary haze. Aimee became aware that her only hope at this point was to get help.

Aimee's wardrobe was a mix of blacks, dark colors, and various shades of grey. She looked good and neat at work, though most of her clothes made her look a bit drab and even at times somber. This may have been fine at the office and at home, yet she already sensed that it would not work for this upcoming meeting and her ongoing work with these new clients.

Jeena had recently been praising the work of an interior designer, Lillian Tam, who was helping Jeena with her new home décor. Lillian was also a well respected personal stylist and feng shui consultant. Jeena had already given her Lillian's phone number suggesting that Lillian could help Aimee with her personal styling — which Jeena had made clear was not to her liking.

Aimee felt skeptical that a personal stylist could really know enough about her to assist her so quickly, and especially to have her ready in time. However, she was desperate enough to give it a try. Aimee had finally given Lillian a call in hopes that Lillian would be available right away.

The next morning precisely on time at ten, Aimee opened her door to a stunning, brightly and elegantly dressed Lillian. Her professional appearance made an immediately favorable impression on Aimee.

Yesterday, Lillian had told Aimee she had an unusual opening, "What an amazing coincidence. I am usually booked full to overflowing, yet tomorrow I happen to have a rare opportunity where I can give you my full attention for the entire day starting at ten."

Aimee had immediately cried, "Yes! Absolutely yes, please come help me."

Now, Aimee heard her own thoughts speaking loudly in her head, "Okay, so there may be something to having a personal style consultation with someone like this woman. She exudes confidence, a bold style, and natural beauty. All attributes I could use."

Extending her hand to Lillian, "I am so happy to meet you." Lillian in turn took Aimee's hand firmly and warmly in hers, "And, I am so happy to meet you as well."

"Lillian, would like you some tea or coffee?"

"Yes, do you have an herbal tea?" Lillian asked as she walked around Aimee's living, dining and kitchen combo room.

"Peppermint work for you?"

"Wonderful. This room is lovely with the high ceilings, tall windows and light openness and the way you've arranged your furniture." Lillian's professional talent for the ancient art of placement immediately recognized Aimee's keen eye for design, color and creating uplifting spaces.

"You've added personal touches to your home in tasteful style and numbers — your glass bowl with rocks and crystals has fabulous color and energy, the photos are well conceived.

"Are these your work? I love the colorful throw pillows and the modern yet comfy look and feel of your furniture. The eclectic styling seems perfect for you. You seem to have a natural intuition about what works well for you and your space."

Lillian then got right to the point, "What about translating this gift into your own body and personal style? What's happened with that? You've told me you wear dark colors and shades of grey, yet your home has complementary blends of bright and darker shades of all the colors of nature."

Lillian had found that many artistic clients could create loveliness around them yet weren't able to translate it to their own appearance.

Aimee looked around her home through Lillian's eyes and understood. When Aimee thought about her closet and what it contained, she hesitated and answered, "I ...don't know."

"Okay," said Lillian. "Since our water has now boiled and the pot is whistling, how about if we make the tea and then sit and we can talk. Plus, I'd like to take a few 'before' photos if that is alright with you."

Chapter 10

WITH STEAMING MUGS OF FRAGRANT PEPPERMINT tea, Aimee and Lillian sat at the well used and cared for oak dining table. Aimee was listening a little skeptically to Lillian's explanations that "fashion can be a work of art worn by someone to enhance their beauty or to alter or conceal it. It's not about the trends. It's about the radiance and glow of health and well-being, creating confidence and self-assuredness, and inspiring loveliness or virile handsomeness.

"Bling and glitter have been incredibly popular. Many people simply like the sparkle. I believe that people are also attracted to the sense of being able to see the stars — to be reminded of the stars in the heavens on a dark night twinkling and winking, beckoning to us. Sometimes, we want to shine like the stars. And, mostly, I think we want to have the hope that our dreams can come true, like the song about when you wish upon a star, your dreams come true.

"So I believe our physical form with its coverings and adornments are really body environments that should be treated with the same sacred respect as the rest of our material universe."

Aimee started considering that maybe she wore predominantly black and grey to make herself seem less visible so that her art and graphic designs would stand out against the plain darkness of her attire. Or, maybe she didn't want draw attention to herself, thinking, "No passion in my wardrobe, no passion with men. Hmm...," She wasn't quite sure, yet she was opening up to what Lillian was saying and willing to give the concepts some merit.

Lillian beamed with her own gentle happiness and continued, "I became a personal stylist and feng shui consultant because I can make a tangible, positive difference in people's lives by helping them with their body, home, office, and other environments.

"I help people honor themselves and see their own intrinsic value and magnificence, offering a little bit of ancient and modern wisdom and advice and helping them align their environments to coincide with who they really are."

Lillian had also suggested that Aimee might like to give an affirmation to confirm herself as the lovely and beautiful person, inside and out, that she really and truly already was. Aimee thought how kindly Lillian had addressed Aimee's lack of self-confidence and assuredness.

After twenty minutes of dialog and taking Aimee's before photos, Aimee began to feel like Lillian was a close friend. Suddenly, uncontrollably emotional, Aimee blurted out everything weighing on her mind in a breathless rush.

"I've just had to clear my entire workload to make room for

a major client, some huge international conglomerate called Holbrook Enterprises, my boss wants to make sure hires us.

"The unusual thing is that apparently the top honcho, Mr. Holbrook himself, asked specifically to have me on the team.

"Usually our project managers, Kristie or Tenzing are the lead. Now Ivan says I will be the lead and other people will be part of the team."

Aimee took a small breath and continued on as though in a hurry to get her thoughts out, "This has me shaking with nerves. Though I feel confident about my abilities to handle graphic design, they want a wide variety of work done which I will have to project manage.

"Ivan has always commented about how I am capable of project management though it sometimes can get in the way of my work as a graphic designer, yet now I will need to be a project manager and only dedicate a portion of my time as a graphic designer. I feel extremely nervous about meeting with the five top executive men who are coming.

"My head is spinning."

Lillian had lightly placed her hand over Aimee's nervously tapping fingers, "Aimee, I'm certain you'll be absolutely fine. Come now and let's look at your clothing."

While they moved toward Aimee's bedroom, Lillian mused with amazement at how the universe worked. She was glad Aimee had let slip the name of the company she was to work with. Lillian already knew a great deal about Holbrook and his company as she had done some interior design and feng shui work at their downtown offices.

Gavin Holbrook himself had wanted to bring tasteful elegance, richness, and nature inside into their executive complex. Lillian smiled remembering how Gavin had become passionately involved in a study of feng shui and consulting with her on how to implement key principles into his environment.

This passion and sharp mind of Gavin's was how he approached everything and how he had brought together an incredible team of men and women who had together created the unparalleled business successes they continued to achieve in the last eight years and now into their ninth year.

Lillian had been genuinely impressed by how the Holbrook men augmented their incredible good looks in natural and authentic ways. They attracted confidence wearing specially tailored business suits with bright colored ties and colored shirts of light blue, golden cream, a gentle rose-red or a soft buttery yellow. Their looks, often of their own unique design, inspired a sense of sophisticated professionalism.

With a deep feeling of satisfaction, Lillian knew with definite certainty that she could help Aimee successfully and confidently meet those dynamic Holbrook men.

They were now in Aimee's bedroom where Lillian had Aimee open her bureau drawers, the door to her walk-in closet and her master bathroom cupboards. Lillian requested Aimee assemble on the bed a couple of complete outfits she might wear to work or consider wearing to meetings with clients, including shoes and accessories.

While Aimee gathered clothes, Lillian wandered into the bathroom. With a keen well-versed eye, she inspected Aimee's array of soaps, creams, makeup, perfumes and sundries. To Lillian there seemed to be a lot of concealer and other cover up creams that could be tossed for Aimee had a loveliness that did not need to be covered over.

Lillian sighed at what she saw and thought to herself, "Oh my, dear Aimee, you are so naturally beautiful. Why are you hiding behind all of this unnatural stuff?

"You have definitely been sold a bill of goods on what might help you look good. Your own golden olive skin, lush brown hair and sparkling hazel eyes are absolutely lovely — just as you are today, completely natural. Well, I'll just need to coax you into allowing your natural beauty to shine and for you to see how authentically gorgeous you truly are."

"I'm ready," came the timid voice of Aimee from the bedroom. When Lillian walked in and saw what was on the bed, with Aimee standing next to it, Lillian immediately recognized Aimee's attempt to hide away her inherent beauty and full bodied figure with her dreary and unbecoming clothes choices.

"Well, Aimee, what's your personal impression of the person who wants to wear these clothes?

"Well, I… um… think she's trying to hide herself. Nothing here seems to want to show off a woman's good figure or to present an upbeat confident person," Aimee timidly replied. "I can't believe how blah and unappealing all this looks.

"Most of my friends and coworkers pretty much avoid wearing all this black and grey, and instead go for bright colors, sparkle and shape hugging styles. Come to think of it, these might be fine going to a funeral or working in a morgue."

Lillian chuckled at Aimee's telling comments and pulled out cloth scarf samples in hundreds of shades of color, much like paint swatch books. "Let's first weed through all your clothes and see what might be salvageable. Then, let's have some fun. You can go through these scarves and pick out colors that you are attracted to and then we can create some color palettes for you."

Hope had taken root and grown as they had gone through every bit of clothing she owned, weeding out more than half of it to be given away to local charities, and seeing how wearing a blend of brighter and richer shades enhanced her looks. Aimee's eyes sparkled with pleasure as they teamed up together and draped colored scarves around her neck.

They were looking at a wide variety of brilliant deep greens, sunny yellows, rich blues and aquas, sparkly gold and silver, vibrant reds and oranges, royal purple, whites and creams, and many subtle hues and shades. Aimee hummed contentedly.

When they had a clear idea of Aimee's preferences and what suited her, Lillian grabbed her large bag, returned into its depths the multitude of scarves now marked with their choices, and hooked Aimee's arm saying, "It's time to go shopping with a stop for lunch. I'm hungry as I imagine you must be as well. There is a small family run French café on the way to the shops."

After they arrived at the café, they found a perfect table near the front windows so they could have the advantage of the natural light. They ordered two of the café's specialty salads and French onion soup with accompanying fresh made baguettes. Homemade fruit tarts completed their lunch selections.

While slowly savoring their flavorful lunches, they

discussed the schedule for the rest of the day and various clothing styles for a professional woman.

"Lillian, the food here is delicious. Now that I know about it, I am coming back and bringing my friends. Everything is so fresh and the fruit tarts are divine," Aimee observed with contentment.

Leaving the café, armed with color swatches and ideas on the cut of clothing that complimented her figure in very professional and positive ways, Lillian and Aimee went shopping. Lillian took Aimee to the uptown exclusive boutique shops where they bought everything — dresses, skirts, pants, shirts, jackets, scarves, and even some exquisitely soft night wear — which was definitely not work related.

Without Aimee's knowledge, Lillian had taken her to a few places Holbrook Enterprises had a large ownership stake in. Lillian was certain there were clothes that would look fabulous on Aimee that the executives might recognize as some of their own labels and designs.

Sure enough, there were dozens of outfits and individual pieces of clothing that looked spectacular on her, and it took a little extra time to make their final selections. Aimee could not remember ever taking so much time to shop, finding so many terrific clothes that looked fantastic on her, or spending so much money on herself.

While at the cash register, Lillian casually asked the cashier about the company and who designed the clothing line. When the cashier mentioned Holbrook Enterprises in among a short list of names, Aimee looked over at Lillian in great surprise. Lillian smiled and then understanding dawned in Aimee which caused a wide smile to grow on her face.

"What a brilliant move, dear Lillian. Thanks a million for your strategic planning. And, I've had a great time with you today. Of course, we've spent a lot of money doing this as well. I can see it is well worthwhile for I feel absolutely wonderful — fantastic in fact."

They spent the next hour treating themselves to a manicure and pedicure. Aimee giggled as it had been awhile since she and her friends had gone out and had a manicure party.

Afterwards Lillian took Aimee to a renowned hair stylist. Aimee had lush, thick tresses that hung down to her waist and was loathe to cut them shorter. The hairdresser recommended a shoulder length cut with sweeping bangs and layers on the sides and in the front. They kept her natural golden brown color and added just a few soft highlights that created an overall shimmering effect.

When the stylist was all done, it was like magic. As Aimee looked in the mirror, she saw how the new hair style brought her best facial features to more prominence and gave her a more professional, and a little bit flirty, look. She swung her head side to side and enjoyed the new feeling of lightness. Aimee was elated that her almost two feet long cut tresses would be donated by the salon to Locks of Love.

Arms loaded with bags and boxes, they returned to Aimee's apartment and continued their work, considering how this would be Aimee's "coming out, moving up and blossoming" event. They worked with simple olive and coconut oils to moisturize her skin and gave her face a soft healthy glow. Lillian gave her dozens of home care tips that would allow for a more natural look and save her quite a bit of money.

Lillian showed Aimee how to blend essential oils to make specific fragrances for use during the day and at night. The addition of a very light undertone of citrus and vanilla seemed to add depth and a unique quality to the jasmine and sandalwood scents already prevalent in her home.

They went through all of Aimee's jewelry and accessories. One of Aimee's friends, Alkisha, was a jewelry designer and had handcrafted some exquisite pieces for Aimee that both Lillian and Aimee thought would effortlessly complement her new wardrobe. Aimee had rarely worn them because they had seemed too bright and sparkly for her. With her new clothes, the jewelry looked fabulous.

At one point during the day she thought she had seen Khan in the distance looking at her with a big smile and a twinkle in his eye. When she had blinked and looked back to where she had seen him, he was gone. In her heart, she knew he had been nearby all day and shared her happiness with her.

Aimee's confidence soared. She became excited about revealing her new image to her co-workers, especially at the Thursday meeting. She could hardly wait to let Khan know how much she appreciated his presence with her today. Long ago, Aimee had established a nightly habit of quietly sitting in her room and telling Khan about her day, letting him know whatever was on her mind or in her heart.

As Lillian was leaving, she turned and asked over her shoulder, "Toodles, and would you like me to come early Thursday morning, as a friend, to help you with your finishing touches? I'll bring my camera."

Aimee was delighted and with eyes glistening, she waved and nodded a vigorous "yes" that caused Lillian to give a happy little laugh.

Chapter 11

THAT NIGHT AFTER A LONG AROMATIC SOAK WITH her favorite beeswax pillar candles burning around the bathroom, a relaxed and loose limbed Aimee readied herself for bed in a new silk, gently clinging, short gown that was modest and yet made her feel thoroughly hugged and softly kissed.

As she laid in bed, Aimee envisioned a successful meeting for the two companies, Signet and Holbrook, and a bright future of collaboration between them. Falling asleep very soon after cozying herself into her comfy bed, she had her best night's sleep in weeks.

While in the shower the next morning, Aimee was singing a song of how wonderful she felt and affirming, "I am confident. I radiate inspiration and professional expertise. My presentation and work with Holbrook Enterprises and my Signet team goes smoothly and fabulously."

Aimee remembered last night that she had visited Khan in his retreat and she told him all about how nervous and uncertain she felt in anticipation of today and asked for his assistance. He had listened and calmed and comforted her.

He had gently asked her, "Aimee, how great are you willing to be?" It now dawned on Aimee that this morning she was feeling more confident. The giving of affirmations and Khan's peaceful presence assisted in calming her. She began to understand what being great meant and the importance of being confident and sure.

Lillian came at eight sharp. Aimee had just started to get dressed. She was scheduled to arrive at the office in a little over an hour to prepare for the eleven o'clock meeting. With expert efficiency, Lillian helped Aimee finish getting dressed in a new outfit she had chosen for today. With Aimee's new hair and glowing face, the softness of her finely tailored peach skirt with complementary jacket over a creamy silk blouse created a dignified elegance. The addition of the intricate swirls and jeweled glitter of her necklace and complimentary earrings created a stunning overall effect.

As soon as Aimee slipped on her soft leather, cream colored heels, Lillian snapped photos of the new Aimee and hurriedly shooed her out the door telling her, "Aimee, you're perfect. I'll lock up. Good luck. Go get 'em."

When Aimee entered the office, she was greeted by eyes popping, jaws dropping and silence when a number of the people in the open air portion of the office saw her enter.

After of a few moments of reverence like quiet, Kristie who was passing through came over to hug Aimee. "You look absolutely amazing! I think it took all of us a few minutes to recognize that it was you." Others rushed over to greet her and exclaimed about how wonderful she looked, complimenting her about her hair, clothes, shoes, jewelry, and her overall look of confidence and radiant beauty.

She walked toward Ivan's office and entered without knocking. Ivan was hunched over concentrating on some paperwork on his desk. "I'm busy."

"Ivan, I hope you are not too busy to look because I don't want you to look shocked when we gather in the conference room."

"What… Aimee? Wow! You look absolutely fantastic! If this meeting is what it took, then it was worth every bit for you to be the lead at this meeting. Go get set up and make sure everyone else who will be in the meeting and the luncheon servers see you beforehand so no one is surprised by your incredible new look."

Chapter 12

Aimee went into the conference room. Even though Signet was a mid-sized company, Ivan had wanted to create an elegant meeting area to attract top-level clients. The soft and dark blues, golds and greens palette created a peaceful, yet energetic place to conduct business. Aimee spritzed the room with a special aromatherapy blend for clear thinking and intuition that served as an air freshener. Breathing deeply of the scent, Aimee felt the freshness and experienced a little boost that the essential oils were designed to convey.

Aimee noticed a glorious arrangement of plants and flowers in the center of the conference table. The delicately sculpted-by-nature blooms were amazing. Everything was carefully placed into a low lying vessel that looked like opalescent mother of pearl, forged out of hand blown crystal. In this way the flowers were low enough not to detract from any conversation or presentation around the table.

She knew this bouquet must have come from their clients. They seemed to have a gift for creating an atmosphere of elegance and inspiration as this spray of flowers seemed to uplift the entire room with its explosion of colors and rich floral scents. Aimee was curious to know if there was a deeper meaning behind this particular arrangement, the specific choice of flowers and colors.

Aimee had raised the level of energy in the room with her aromatic spray and they had done it with the flower arrangement. Truly, they would make a dream team together.

Finished with her room preparations, Aimee went back to her office to gather her materials and her laptop for her Power Point introduction. She had created a graphically rich presentation that she hoped everyone would find informative and interesting.

Right at eleven, Aimee entered the conference room which was now abuzz with the other eleven people in the room already. She was greeted by her office mates, and looking around the room, she noticed a man who stood facing and looking out the windows at the back of the room, powerful hands clasped behind his back. Something seemed vaguely familiar about the tall, broad shouldered silhouette. In that moment, he turned to her with a broad knowing smile.

"Gavin!" Aimee exclaimed. "Are you a part of Holbrook Enterprises?"

With a deep chuckle, Connor glanced over at Gavin and then to Aimee and remarked, "Ah, so you know Gavin. Aimee, this is Gavin Holbrook."

Aimee put her hand on the table to steady herself, whispering under her breath, "Gavin Holbrook. Oh… my… yes, glad to meet you."

When she looked at Gavin in a foggy shock, she recognized his finely sculpted features and rich darkly colored hair and eyes from their encounter in the hallway. His warm gaze had her feeling her toes tingle.

In her mind she called out, "Yikes. Oh, Khan please help with this entire presentation and meeting. Why is this particular man involved?"

Hot tea and coffee was being served around the table. Aimee turned to look to her left and noticed that Gavin's eyes were drawn there as well. Aimee released a quiet sound of surprise and pleasure as she saw Khan standing to the side of the room absolutely resplendent in his familiar electric blue over garment.

What was new to Aimee was that his turban was adorned with a large sparkling, crystal clear blue diamond. He held his hands at chest level where his heart radiated an intense rose pink light that intensified and expanded out to encompass the entire room. Aimee felt enfolded in a comforting warmth. Aimee whispered in her heart saying no words aloud, "Thank you, dear Khan."

She rejoiced in seeing his magnanimous smile and saw his love and support of her in his eyes. As always, he made her feel cherished, valued and full of hope. She knew she was completely loved and in that instant knew that what was happening around her was her destiny and that she must follow her heart and intuition — deciding for herself her courses of action for the future. He showered her with a keen awareness of singular purpose and to honor him by doing her genuine best.

Khan had consistently made it clear that he could not and

would not make decisions for her and that she needed to be empowered to gain her own victories and her heart's desires. She knew if he gave her too much direction, the successful outcomes would be his and not hers. He was firmly setting her on a journey of self-realization and achievement and supporting her through her own choices.

She seemed to be suspended in time where what passed in a few seconds had felt like many minutes. As Khan faded from view, Aimee's attention returned to the conversations around the table as the tea and coffee service was nearing a close. She caught Gavin's eyes shift from where Khan had stood to her with slightly raised eyebrows. Aimee noticed how a little something undecipherable momentarily flickered in his expressive eyes. The glint passed quickly, and he returned to his natural acumen, native to this internationally renowned business guru.

Aimee's stomach churned as her excitement and a bit of nervousness took over. "What will this meeting bring? Why had Khan appeared with such imperial dignity and given such a tremendous blessing?"

She took a deep calming breath and began. "Thank you everyone for gathering today. On behalf of Signet Marketing, I would like to welcome all of you from Holbrook Enterprises." Her authentic welcome showed in her smile and eyes as she greeted each of the good looking and impeccably dressed executives around the table.

Though Aimee's five-ten height kept her at eye level with people at over six feet even when seated, however, the Holbrook men still seemed to tower over everyone at the table.

The sheer breadth of wide muscular torsos and broad shoulders gave an awe inspiring impression.

This powerhouse of five of the most virile males she had ever seen together like this caused her a little trepidation as she spoke, "We are looking forward to working as a collaborative team together with you for the success of your company projects."

She turned herself fully to the right to face Gavin asking, "Mr. Holbrook, would you like to start us off by introducing your team and your vision of what we might be able to assist you with?"

He noticed Aimee's courageous determination to stay calm. "Aimee Beaumont, I am Gavin Mansur Holbrook. The pleasure is ours to meet you. You can call me Gavin." His eyes sparkled with mischievous humor as his lips quirked with a smile.

He then introduced the other four Holbrook executives, Connor, Ahmed, Hawk, and John. The five men radiated power and dignity. Each one of their smiles shone with genuine and sincere warmth as they shook hands with everyone.

The Scot, Connor, had glistening red hair, soft freckles, sparkling hazel green eyes, and an upturned mouth as though he was always smiling. Connor laughed easily and heartily.

Ahmed, the Indian prince, may have been the shortest at five-ten yet his countenance was just as commanding as the others. Ahmed's warm smile radiated from his rich dark brown face. His peaceful demeanor had a calming effect on Aimee.

Hawk was the tallest and most imposing looking with

broad shoulders and taut, muscular chest and abdomen. His raven hair hung to below his wide shoulders and seemed to soften his sharply chiseled Native American features. His mellow toned greeting, "Nice to meet all of you" and natural charm warmed the hearts of Aimee and her team.

He turned a keen eye to Aimee, perused her outfit and complimented her, "Lovely outfit. Seems familiar. Looks stupendous on you!" His comment grabbed the immediate attention of his friends.

Aimee countered with, "Yes, thank you. I love the design. A friend of mine took me to a place that you may know, Opportunité Emporium. Right?"

John sounded a hearty, "We sure do, though I'm certain those clothes never looked as good as they look on you." Aimee's cheeks pinkened at his praise.

John appeared as a Greek god-like man — tall, broad, blonde, crystal clear blue eyes, and golden tanned. Aimee sensed he knew how handsome he was yet kept himself from being arrogant or too proud of it. When she had looked into his eyes, the clarity of them made her feel that she was looking into the depths of his soul.

Hawk had graciously explained to the Signet staff that the Holbrook company owned a majority interest in the store that carried the clothes Aimee had bought and owned one of the main designer labels of clothing and accessories at Opportunité.

During the interchange, Aimee's eyes wandered to gauge Gavin's reaction. Earlier, she had noticed that he had gingerly gazed over her with a look of pleasure and joy. His handsome face, an excellent blend of the best features of his English and Arabic origins, now held a wide sheepish grin. She quickly averted her eyes to others in the room.

In a very short time any sense of nervousness or trepidation evaporated as everyone began to enjoy each other's professional and business diplomacy and good humor.

Aimee smiled broadly as she noticed that with her team, the group of twelve in the conference room looked as though they were representatives from various nations getting together — Ivan's evident Russian background and accent, Tenzing's Tibetan heritage, Kristie's Southeast Asian beauty, Robby's handsome African features, and Aislinn's classic black Irish looks. Aimee, with her French and a little Spanish background, felt such pleasure at the diversity and the high level of integrity and professionalism of everyone meeting together.

For the next few hours, a lively discussion ensued about both companies and the projects Holbrook wanted Signet to work on for them, particularly some advertising and marketing pieces for a new fashion house they had recently acquired. When the company events planner lightly knocked and announced that lunch was ready for them, it was the perfect moment to switch locations.

Little clusters of people were deeply engaged in various conversations while enjoying a delicious luncheon. The caterers had prepared a fantastic meal — from the tender, fresh locally grown greens in the salad to the expertly prepared entree options that catered to the various tastes of different people in the room.

While the main lunch dishes were being cleared and

dessert was being given to each person, Aimee asked everyone to applaud the work of their events planner and the owners of the catering company, who had done their homework in finding out what each person in the room liked beforehand and then prepared individual entrees for each.

Dessert was a delicious looking, smelling and tasting concoction of coconut milk, fresh vanilla bean, delicate flower petals, organic fruit, a little tapioca, a squeeze of lemon, a touch of sweetener and fresh mint. Everyone was able to indulge, and there were many requests for the recipe. John had dubbed it "ambrosia of the gods."

They adjourned from the body-and-soul satisfying lunch back to the conference room where over the next two hours more and more details, including a variety of projects involved, their scope, budget ideas and time lines, were tossed around.

A running document was being logged as well as a multitude of drawings and illustrations on a number of computer note pads were being stored for reference.

Kristie, who had volunteered to be note taker and to try and keep them on track, consistently asked for clarification and periodically reviewed her summaries with everyone to ensure she had everything correctly documented.

There was quite a bit of humor and good will around the table. Work group teams had already been starting to develop. Aimee thought that it was clearly evident that the people from both companies were an excellent match for working together.

The first major project they agreed to pursue together included online and print advertising for one of their biochemical research firms. A lot of notes had been taken about the details for Aimee to get a good start.

Chapter 13

To her boss, co-workers and friends at Signet Marketing, Aimee had always epitomized professional honesty, hard work, creativity, diligence and deep caring for people. She had planned to stay this way in her work for Holbrook Enterprises.

For the next few weeks Aimee was busy with the Holbrook project. Instead of staying focused, Aimee found herself starting to get a bit scattered and sometimes feeling overwhelmed. Irked with herself, she blamed him, Gavin, for distracting her because it seemed visions of his warm brown eyes and ready smile assailed her.

She chided herself because first, she had vowed to never get romantically involved with a client or a co-worker. Second, she just had a breakup with Chad and needed time to heal over that. And, lastly, her thoughts seemed to drift into planning how she would maintain a neutral relationship with the debonair Mr. Holbrook during her work with his company.

"I'm spending too much time thinking about him," Aimee concluded as she willed herself to stop.

Since she was working primarily with Connor and other members of their company team, she had not had to confront the issue of Gavin directly. She pointedly focused on creating the variety of brochures and marketing tools they had requested.

When Aimee satisfactorily completed drafts of all the materials and concepts for every aspect of this project, she had gone over everything with Connor. He expressed his approval and looked forward to going over it all with his team to get their feedback.

Over the last few weeks, Aimee had become fast friends with all but one of the confident and powerful Holbrook men. She had worked closely with Connor, John, Ahmed and Hawk on her projects getting their ideas and input. Conveniently, Aimee had managed to avoid Gavin as he had been in New York.

Connor told Aimee with a smile of appreciation, "We are so pleased to be working with you. You are an incredibly gifted designer. Once these are approved, will your team be able to assist you to complete all the details?"

"Yes, Ivan has committed people to it." Aimee informed Connor.

"Good. Gavin and I would like to speak with you privately on other matters of interest."

Connor's words left Aimee feeling excitement and a little trepidation, especially at the prospect of more work with the Holbrook team.

"Thanks, Connor. My main contributions to these projects are close to finished. I have a little more creative work to accomplish once you give direction on some of these mock-ups. Then, I will be able to pass the work to our production teams to complete. I will be free to work on any new assignments with you," Aimee answered with spontaneous eagerness.

Eyebrows arched in amusement, Connor noted Aimee's surprise at her own evident enthusiasm. Chuckling, Connor could only say enigmatically, "There is much more to come between you and our Holbrook team."

Over the weekend Aimee mulled over Connor's mysterious statement and the possible meaning behind it. She knew she would have to wait until Monday after she received their feedback to try and ferret out what Connor and the rest of the Holbrook team had in mind.

Chapter 14

MONDAY MORNING, GAVIN ENTERED THE SIGNET Marketing offices with Connor and Priscilla who had come from the New York research office where Gavin had been. He reminisced that today was a little over three weeks since he had seen Aimee. He had thought of her often in anticipation of seeing her again.

Now, today he was determined to discover if he truly had authentic feelings for Aimee in the way he had been imagining or if it was a mental illusion with no true substance. He was here to approve her work and to set up a time when the Holbrook execs could discuss some ideas that they had been discussing as ways they could help her. He had also held a little selfish hope that one of his newly reawakened dreams might be attainable in the near future as well.

The office was abuzz with activity. Ivan had told Gavin that a flood of new jobs had come in at the same time that Holbrook had brought their projects to them. Though Gavin was glad of this, as he liked to see local companies growing successfully, he wanted to make sure Aimee would be able to concentrate on their assignments.

Kristie greeted Gavin, Connor, and Priscilla as they entered the office and directed them to the conference room. "I'll get Aimee and Tenzing and be right back."

When the three entered a few moments later, Gavin's eyes quickly greeted Tenzing and then darted over to fully rest on watching Aimee. When her eyes met his, he felt a charge in the air and the strong connection he had known he had with her. The air between them sparked with attraction.

Gavin realized he was totally and utterly smitten, confirming to himself, "There is no doubt about it. I have answered my own question. I am inextricably connected to Aimee."

Shock registered on Aimee as she felt a tingling all over, and she thoughtfully mused to herself, "I need to remain strong, detached. Falling for this guy is totally impractical. He's way out of my league, and besides, I want to focus on my business. His company may be willing to assist me, but it's my work that will make it a success. Gavin is a distraction — a big hunk of one."

Aimee tore her gaze from Gavin and looked at Connor who introduced her to Priscilla. For the next two hours, the six of them went through the fine points of each of the pieces of work and came to complete agreement on everything.

After Connor, Gavin and Priscilla had given their final approvals and had risen to leave, Gavin turned to Aimee and inquired in a whisper, "Would you join Connor and me with the rest of our executive team for dinner tomorrow night in celebration — and also for us to discuss some important matters with you?" Gavin inhaled deeply of her sandalwood, citrus, and jasmine scent and watched her breathing becoming more rapid at his closeness and whispered words.

"I, ah, …I could come. Yes, that would be fine. Where? Seven, right?" Aimee stammered out barely above a whisper.

"I will come to your office and get you at six. We'll be going to Nellie and Jake's Diner so it's casual dress. Is that okay?"

"Oh … okay…"

Gavin left her standing on the inside of the front door as he had walked out. Aimee questioned her own sanity in accepting dinner with Gavin even if four others would be there with them. She found that she was not as immune to his charms as she thought.

Chapter 15

GAVIN FOUND AIMEE PACING BACK AND FORTH NEAR the front entryway with a bemused look on her lovely face. He liked how she looked in a gently hugging green top that had a hint of glitter, and he recognized it as part of their line, tucked into her belted, snug fitting jeans. She carried a lovely blue and green sweater over her arm that like it would keep her warm in the chill of the evening.

When Gavin entered and called a greeting to Aimee, she noticeably started. He wondered if something was troubling her. "Aimee, a penny for your thoughts," suggested Gavin gently.

"Oh, Gavin, it's you. I was deep in thought, wasn't I?" Aimee's eyes showed a little wariness and doubt. Gavin wondered if she was being cautious of him or her own self.

"Are you set to go? The others are already at the diner. They've said you've all become friends over the last three weeks working together."

"Yes, we have, and I'm ready and feel quite hungry now." Aimee seemed to gain back some of her spark and walked out the front door patting her flat tummy to emphasis her need for food.

When Gavin pulled into a parking space, he shrugged his shoulders and turned to Aimee with a wide grin lighting his face explaining, "Here's our favorite diner. The pool tables are really great fun, and the food is exceptional."

Laughing at the thought of playing pool for the first time with these five probable pool sharks, Aimee could only choke out a weak, "okay" as she got out of the car to go in. In the waning light, Aimee could see the parking lot was full of vehicles of all models, shapes and sizes. This was obviously a hopping place, especially for a Tuesday night.

Entering the diner, Aimee could see into the large cavern in the back where there were quite a number of pool tables, and saw that the entire place was packed to overflowing.

The delicious smells of burgers, fries, fresh baked bread, muffins and pies, turkey and gravy and who knows what else assaulted her senses and caused her to salivate. Now, Aimee really felt hungry.

"Shall we eat first? Or play first?"

"Eat first."

Gavin laughed good-naturedly at Aimee's quick fire response. He expertly steered them to the very farthest back corner where he opened a door into a small private dining room where the others were busy munching chips and dip. All of them rose at once to greet one another and Aimee with sincere pleasure. Connor and John applauded her work and greeted her enthusiastically.

Right away they offered Gavin and Aimee seats with a

frosty glass of lemonade in place for each of them. Aimee drank deeply of the refreshing tangy drink, downing half of her glass. "This is wonderful! Lemonade with a bit of bubble?"

Gavin explained that they had made a pact very early in their careers as young entrepreneurs to avoid anything that dulled their thinking, dampened their senses, or diminished their intuitive abilities. They had come up with a refreshing, zesty lemonade drink and shared their recipe with places they frequented.

All of the men had divested themselves of jackets, ties and any other accessories. Collars were opened relieving confined necks, and shirt sleeves were rolled up to display well toned hands and arms. Everyone seemed to relax. Aimee had worn a soft sweater that she added to the pile lying on an open chair.

The conversation around the dining table became boisterous and animated, covering a dizzying array of subjects. Aimee tried with minimal success to follow the flow of discussions swirling around her.

The waitress, a good looking woman with graying blonde hair, came in. She called out, "You, hot shot boys, are you showing off for this nice looking young lady here? You want your usual? Today's special is meatloaf, you know, with mashed potatoes and lots of our yummy gravy."

John whined teasingly with a silly puppy faced expression, "Ah, LaVerne darling, now don't give us a bad rap. You know how charming and well behaved we really are."

LaVerne's laughter rang out throughout the room, and everyone joined in. They ordered a complete round for everyone of the special in addition to their usual of burgers, hot dogs and fries. Aimee thought that it was going to be a mountain of food.

When the plates were delivered, Aimee saw she was right — the portions were huge and the table overflowed with a great deal of wonderfully smelling, diner fare. The conversation died down as everyone hungrily dug in.

In short order the food piles were demolished and the men began to discuss what would happen next. A toast was called by Hawk who then thanked Aimee, Connor and Gavin for their commendable work together. And, then Hawk was pulling Aimee up from the table saying that it was time for some games of pool.

Aimee had never been with a more friendly, good-natured and teasing group of men while they played fast paced rounds of pool. They did not even seem to be able to count or keep their own ball colors or patterns straight as they played nine-ball and eight-ball pool games. She could not remember laughing so hard over silly comments and game plays.

At one point Hawk had even laid on the table trying to get his ball in an end pocket while the others had hooted and hollered. They drank only their special lemonade, as was their habit, and were able to act fully uninhibited and overflowing with fun and life while keeping their mind's sharp. Aimee was completely swept up in their merriment.

They attracted a great deal of attention from others in the restaurant and pool hall. There were a number of good looking women who came over and flirted outrageously with the men, especially Gavin and Connor, both of whom were without wedding rings. A couple of voluptuous blondes had draped themselves over the two bachelors.

Though both Connor and Gavin had quickly and graciously disentangled themselves, Aimee felt an unexpected twinge of irritation at Gavin. She decided to dismiss her irrational feelings as nonsense as she did not have any hold on him nor was she willing to admit that she had any attraction to the man.

After shaking herself from continuing to picture the women hanging onto these men, Aimee paid close attention to how the men talked of serious business matters in the midst of their gaming. She marveled at their ability to conduct a meeting while joking and playing around. She was duly impressed with their astute business acumen. They were also extremely gifted in how they drew her in and made her feel a natural part of their camaraderie.

"It's time for pie," shouted John over the music in the pool hall.

"Let's go…" trailed Ahmed's voice behind him as he led the way back into their dining room.

The room was now set up with several fresh baked and still warm pies — cherry, apple, peach, banana cream and some other yummy looking delectables. Vanilla ice cream, fresh fruit and whipped cream were on hand. These men seemed to know exactly what they wanted for their desserts.

After everyone had a delicious plate in front of them, the conversation turned into a review of all that they had discussed and decided in the pool room and determining who was responsible for what actions. John was entering some notes into his iPad. Aimee was once again keenly aware that they had kept clear and precise recollections of all their discussions in their heads — from the dinner table as they ate with gusto, through their pool playing antics and the loud music and noise in the pool hall. After twenty minutes of their dialogue, the conversation took a totally different turn.

All five men turned to look directly at Aimee. The intensity of these ten eyes on her made her squirm. Aimee turned to look at Gavin who had started in his smooth voice, "Aimee, we five would like to offer you our personal and company assistance in helping you set up your own business. We would like to be one of your clients. We can continue to give a few projects to Signet in appreciation of the work you have done for us through them.

"My grandaunt Bertie told me of your dream to create your own graphic design and web development company. We have discussed this and believe we can assist you in a number of ways."

Hawk piped up next, "Our legal and financial offices have a great deal of experience and can give you advice."

Connor added, "And, we can share our business experience with you. Plus, we have a wide variety of connections, and if you desire, we can send clients your way."

Aimee was wide eyed with amazement and her eyes were glistening with tears. She was speechless. Gavin caught Aimee's attention and asked, "Will you let us help you? We want so much to be able to do so."

"Don't cry." Aimee told herself. "Especially not now in front of these incredible men."

"Aimee, are you alright?" Gavin asked.

What Aimee could say came out barely audible, "How can I ever thank all of you? This means so much to me I can hardly even speak, and I'm having trouble not becoming overly emotional right now."

"Please allow me to thank you on all of our behalf," Ahmed acknowledged, "We are grateful for the excellence of your work with us. Besides wanting to help you establish your own business, we have an additional selfish motive for wanting you to be on your own.

"We want to ask if you would be willing to have Holbrook Enterprises as your first major, and initially exclusive, client.

"And, if in six weeks, you would be able to travel with Connor, Gavin, my wife and me on business to India for four months. We have a number of vital ventures and associations in India. My wife and I have family there who we will visit as well. And, all of us are invited to the wedding of friends and associates of ours in New Delhi."

Ahmed continued, "This will be an all expenses paid trip. The company will pay for your flights, travel, food and lodging. You will only need money to buy souvenirs or little things for yourself. You will tour some of our facilities. If you are willing, we would like you to take on a few design projects for our Indian companies while we are there. And, of course, you will be given plenty of time to be a tourist as well and visit some of the sites and wonders of India. I know Ayesha will love to take you wherever you'd like to go."

Aimee's astonishment grew throughout Ahmed's discourse. "India?" the surprise and hesitation in Aimee's voice was evident. "I've never been to India. I've hardly ever traveled outside of the United States. When I was young, we went to France a few times to visit my grandparents. That's the only faraway place I've traveled to before."

Gavin added softly, noticing Aimee's hesitation, "Aimee, I know it may seem overwhelming right now. Just take a little time to think about it. Consider taking this chance, letting us help you create your own business, and coming with us to India."

When Aimee looked around the room at the happiness and welcome of these five kind men, tears of joy escaped down her cheeks. She could only nod and rasp out, "Oh, how can I ever thank you? How could I ever deserve so much? And, can this really be truly happening for me?"

"Yes, it's real!" came the united exclamation of all five deeply rich male voices as they all grinned at her.

"Aimee, let me take you home now." Gavin offered gently. "Please think about these offers. We are all united in wanting you to become part of our business team. We will meet again with more details." Gavin had grabbed his tie and jacket and her sweater and was leading her out to the car.

Chapter 16

THE RIDE HOME HAD BEEN IN COMPANIONABLE silence. Aimee had forgotten that Gavin knew where she lived. As Gavin was slowing the car to park in a space in front of her building, Aimee had bounded from his car, hurled a thank you, and rushed to her apartment.

Gavin battled his utter surprise at Aimee's hasty disappearance from him. He was not sure what she really thought of their offers. Even though he knew he needed to give her a little time and space, he wished she would confide in him. He decided he would wait patiently until Friday, and then, if she had not called him, he would contact her.

Friday evening Gavin rang the doorbell to Aimee's apartment. None of them had heard a word from Aimee. Gavin had come to plead their company, and his, case.

"Gavin, it's you. Please come in." Aimee hesitated. "I apologize that I have not gotten back with you. That's why you came, right?"

"Yes, Aimee."

"Okay, we'll talk. Please come in and have a seat. I was making myself some popcorn with real butter. Would you like some?"

"Smells wonderful. Popcorn would be great."

Bringing bowls filled with the buttery, fresh popped kernels into the living room, Aimee handed Gavin a bowl and sat across from him in one of her comfy overstuffed chairs.

"Gavin, I'm truly grateful for your wonderful proposals. I've been a bit overwhelmed with it all. I guess in part I don't really believe I deserve it."

"Of course, you do, Aimee. We want you to come with us to India. There will be work to do and celebrations to attend. You can get fresh new ideas and see what inspires you when traveling in another country and culture." Gavin spoke softly.

The sound of his voice soothed Aimee. She thought, "Oh no, he's trying to seduce me into agreeing to go." She determined to stand firm against Gavin's charm and any personal seduction attempts by him. But then, he wove more of his enchantment. "Here is a handmade silk sari for you. This silk is made in Bhoodhan Pochampally, also known as the Silk City, and is some of the finest silk available anywhere on earth. These saris are made by our silk artisans and weavers there. That is one of the areas we plan to visit."

Aimee experienced pleasure as the silk shimmered smoothly over her arms and hands. The fine weave and softness was beyond description. She turned to Gavin, eyes sparkling with delight.

In that moment, as though veils lifted clearing her vision, Aimee knew she must seize this chance for herself. She wanted to spread her wings and the thought of experiencing the exotic land of India, steeped in a culture and traditions unfamiliar to her, was tantalizing. She knew she had to break free of her own past limiting beliefs about herself. And, she planned to avoid Gavin.

With restrained eagerness, Aimee answered, "Yes, I have thought deeply about this. I realize this is an incredible opportunity for me so I'll go with you…er…your company."

Apparently not noticing her slip of the tongue at the end, joy shone brightly on Gavin's face. When Aimee had glanced his way, he had given her an excited smile. She quickly turned away, doubting herself around this man.

Gavin left soon after Aimee announced her decision. He had immediately gone to grandaunt Bertie's to share his good news with her. She simply listened, smiled and embraced him warmly. He had stayed only briefly because he was in a rush to contact Connor and Ahmed to set their plans in motion.

Chapter 17

Jeena sat on Aimee's couch and listened to Aimee rant about the idea of having to travel with Gavin, especially since he expected her to accompany him to both business and personal events. The others going to India would be there most of the time, yet Aimee was still concerned about being around Gavin. Her nails were taking a beating as she gnawed on them as a dog with a bone would. She had never been known to bite her nails.

"What am I to do?" Aimee was lamenting. "I just can't be around him so much, as he looks at me as though he wishes to eat me alive or even more so to ravish me on the spot. It makes me shiver and shake. I grow hot and then cold and goosebumpy all over. What is wrong with me?"

"Nothing is wrong with you. And, why can't you be around him? When I checked him out online, that man looked simply delicious. Didn't Chad think you needed more passion in your life? Seems to me that your Mr. Holbrook is bringing it out in you."

"Bah, humbug. Passion seems overrated. After all, I meet him and soon after, I'm thinking about what kissing him would be like. Yuck. Doesn't seem like anything other than a little nonsensical physical attraction to me. No one talks about lust at first sight being the same as love at first sight.

"He can have any woman he wants. They literally throw themselves at him. So, he can't possibly want someone like me. And, I am certainly not interested in some shallow, male hormone boosting fling."

Flustered, Jeena felt ready to give Aimee a good shake. "Oh Aimee, for heaven's sake! You're being ridiculous. I see perfectly why Gavin could easily be attracted to your phenomenal self. Why can't you? Quit putting yourself down and trying to excuse yourself from your feelings. That's really a bunch of hogwash, Aimee, and you know it!

"Besides, I'd like to remind you that with a man and a woman love can express itself in many ways, including affection, passionate kissing and more. After all, that's how babies are born." Jeena was chuckling at her own telling.

"Jeena!" screeched Aimee. "How can you say such things at a time like this."

With a chortle and in a whisper Jeena answered, "So you see how love grows with passion inside of you for someone. Grab your happiness, dear Aimee. Strike while the iron's hot. Carpe diem. Your Mr. Holbrook just might be the one for you to share love, passion and happiness with."

"Well, he may not even want me. Oh, what am I to do?" sighed Aimee who continued to have a look of grave concern across her face while she distractedly unraveled the yarn at the edge of her sweater cuff.

Jeena answered, "You won't know unless you try."

Chapter 18

AIMEE HAD ALWAYS BELIEVED THAT HER NATURAL joie de vivre had helped her transition through many of life's trials, and even her past successes. She had lived by the motto that where there is a will, there is a way. But, for some reason neither had helped her with her relationships.

There had to be a way for this trip to be amazing and fun for her. Directly confronting her turbulent emotions about being around Gavin Holbrook for what she had counted as one hundred and twenty-two days, she devised a survival plan.

Talking about this with herself, she had concluded, "Aimee, you love art. India is abundantly rich with spectacular art and architecture you have never seen before. What about coming up with places you can visit on your own or with a guide while the men are busy elsewhere? They said you could go touring, so why not take them up on their offer in a big way?"

Aimee felt back in charge of her own life again. She resolved to pay close attention at their meeting, taking notes on exactly where they were going, and then do some of her own research as to places she might be interested in touring in each location.

A few days later, a focused Aimee met with Connor, Ahmed and Gavin on their itinerary for the India trip. The plan included arriving in Bangalore, the 'Silicone Valley' of India.

They would be primarily focused in the city with a few trips to other nearby areas, including to Bhoodhan Pochampally, the Silk City where the exquisite sari Gavin had given her had been made.

After being in southern India for six weeks, they would head north to the sprawling metropolis of Delhi, primarily focused in the national capital city of New Dehli, for the remaining ten weeks.

During their time in the Dehli area, Aimee would be able to visit the Taj Mahal in Agra. Ahmed had offered that Ayesha would be happy to be her tour guide. They listed a couple of other business trips to be taken in northern India. One had Aimee goose-bumped with excitement.

While Ahmed and Ayesha remained in New Dehli, Gavin and Connor were scheduled for a ten-day excursion to the Darjeeling region. They had asked if Aimee would like to accompany them. She had spontaneously jumped up, done a little dance, and shouted with jubilation, "Yes! Darjeeling, yes!"

Gavin, Connor, and Ahmed were taken by complete surprise and now eyed her with astonishment showing in their expressions.

"Oops, sorry, I guess I got a little carried away. It's just… well…"

Keeping from outright laughing, an amused Ahmed explained, "Aimee, it's fine. That was quite a little dance. We're actually very happy to see you so excited." Then, everyone broke out in full laughter that rippled throughout the entire room.

During the merriment, a fleeting thought crossed Aimee's mind that her enthusiasm for going to Darjeeling had to do with Khan, and maybe this would be a pilgrimage of sorts to Khan's retreat.

Somehow she had always known that his dwelling was in the Himalayas in Darjeeling, though it seemed more ethereal than physical. She had never imagined that she might be able to visit there.

Connor had gone on to describe that Darjeeling was famous for its pungent teas with an estimated one hundred and forty-four tea gardens, pristine lakes, waterfalls, hiking trails, markets, and local trade. From there they offered to take Aimee on an overnight tour of a little of the famous Sikkim region. They would return to New Dehli for their friends' wedding celebration prior to returning home.

On a large screen note pad, Connor had traced their entire route showing spectacular photos, a few maps and video clips of the regions where they would be going and places they would stay.

Connor looked inquiringly at Aimee and asked, "This trip we will miss going to Mumbai. We won't be able to tour Bollywood as we will be short of time. Would you be terribly disappointed? Many people like to travel there when going to India."

"As you can probably now guess, I am much more interested in going to where you are already scheduled to go. Thank you so much." Knowing she had touring plans of her own, Aimee flashed Connor a huge grin and leaned over to deliver a light nudge with her hand on his hard muscled upper arm.

She considered Connor a brother. All of the Holbrook founders felt like brothers, though there was still something a bit different about her feelings toward Gavin. She kept experiencing odd sensations around him. She had decided not to dwell on it, and instead focus on the incredible journey to India.

Gratitude for this miraculous opportunity glowed in Aimee's face. She turned a dazzling smile and eyes sparkling with joy toward Connor, Ahmed and Gavin.

Gavin's eyes filled with a triumphant expression. He spoke with a deliberately measured rhythm as if to impress the importance of his words onto Aimee's soul, "I am honored. For it is my pleasure to have you share this journey with me."

Eyes locked, Aimee felt light-headed and giddy. She questioned herself again for what seemed like the umpteenth time, "How am I going to keep myself from getting entangled with this man while spending months with him? He is driving me crazy with his arrogant charm."

Chapter 19

AIMEE'S FRIENDS HAD DECIDED THEY WANTED TO know first-hand what was going on with Aimee. Only bits and pieces had filtered through to each of them. Katy arranged for all the girls to meet at her house.

As the six friends gathered bearing scrumptious potluck dishes, Aimee was scheduled to arrive after her other friends had laid out the smorgasbord feast. The anxious looks on the faces of Jeena, Katy, Alkisha, Hope, Gabriella, Liza and another lifelong friend who had not been part of the original camp group, Suze, showed their deep concerns about Aimee.

When Jeena told them of her conversation with Aimee from a few days ago, the story produced a little relieved laughter through the group. Suze interjected with joyous glee, "Aimee certainly deserves the love and attention of a fine man."

Moments later Aimee walked in the front door and felt the unspoken love of all her friends. Greeting them and dropping heavily with an anguished sigh into the nearest available comfy chair, Aimee burst into tears.

Everyone reacted immediately by surrounding her with hugs, trying to comfort her and stop her tears.

"Thank you, my dear friends, these are tears mixed with joy and anxiety. I just don't know what to think anymore."

"Why don't you finish your tears and then we can eat to give you strength for the telling of your story," Hope gently coaxed.

Hope was true to her name and was the one who seemed to stay the most calm and hopeful during times of turmoil, especially during some of the most fierce battles with rebellious kids at camp.

"Okay," a little sob sounded from Aimee.

After a few more minutes, all of them went to enjoy the potluck meal, filling plates and bringing them into the living room.

Between swallows, Aimee began to relate her awe inspiring tale beginning in her rooftop garden to when the Holbrook executives had offered to assist her in establishing her own company and take her on a trip to India with Gavin, Connor and Ahmed and his wife.

There were many sighs and smiles around the room from her friends as they enjoyed Aimee's stories. Liza added detailed descriptions of the five men. She had met Gavin, Connor, John, Hawk and Ahmed at a fund-raising gala that she had attended.

Liza used her lithe body to create animated pictorial portraits of each of the men, showing their full height and breadth, the fine features of each of their faces and their muscular and powerful builds. Liza's accurate renditions caused great amusement and some serious drooling, with even a little among Aimee's married friends. As Jeena had once said, "Any woman can appreciate the look of a well sculpted man as a fine piece of art, as a magnificent artistic creation —whether married or not. It's well known how men appreciate beautiful women in this way."

Her friends helped her recognize that some of her anxiety had to do with wanting to impress the Holbrook company with her abilities and that she needed to remain confident of her own creative inspirations. Dealing with her feelings toward Gavin was merely a part of the total picture of forging her ongoing work relationship with the company.

The camaraderie and close bond of these eight women was tangible as they galvanized to decide action plans and who would help Aimee with planning, shopping, packing, organizing, and all the rest she had to accomplish in the next few weeks. Everyone volunteered to pitch in, and everyone was ready to move into action.

The first thing on Aimee's list was to talk with Ivan. That very afternoon Aimee gave him notice about quitting her job at Signet Marketing. Ivan had commented in his pleasant tone of voice, "Well, I was expecting your call, though I can't say I'm happy about losing you . I am thrilled for you about your own business and your impending trip to the East.

"John gave me a little warning that they were going to propose you establish your own business and take this trip to India with them. Aimee, dear, I am very, very happy for you. Please keep in touch. I'll just need you to come in and check on the progress of the current Holbrook projects in their production phases and to clear your office area."

In the evening Aimee had already planned to join her parents and brother for dinner so she could let them know her exciting news about going to India. Her parents and Paul were ecstatic for her. Her parents were both were well traveled in Europe, the Middle East and Asia. Paul had been on several missionary trips to Africa and Southeast Asia so he knew what a life changing experience travel could be.

Much of Aimee's time over the next ten days was spent with Suze who had been able to accompany her to renew her passport, update her shots, and go with her to dental and other appointments.

Lillian had also come by a few times to assist her with wardrobe and accessories and to give her good luck hugs and blessings. Katy, Jeena, Liza, Gabriella, Hope and Alkisha all pitched in to help Aimee in every way possible.

Her parents and brother Paul were an incredible support as well and had given her new luggage, some extra spending money and a couple of nifty compression bags that allowed her to compact her clothing into smaller spaces.

Gabriella had volunteered to tend Aimee's rooftop garden while she was away. Gabriella was a sous-chef at a premier restaurant. The executive chef was her boyfriend — hopefully soon to be fiancée. They enjoyed using the freshest vegetables and herbs from local organic markets, including those grown by their restaurant and on occasion Aimee's greenhouse.

Bertie had found out Aimee was going on this company

trip to India from her grandnephew Gavin and offered to check on Aimee's apartment now and then as she was right next door. Bertie had met Aimee's friends, Jeena, Hope and Gabriella while they had helped in the gardens and knew they would be coming around to work in the gardens and would need to use Aimee's apartment to change and clean up.

More than once Aimee had expressed tears of gratitude for all the tender care and consideration of her friends and family. And, she shared frequent hugs of warm appreciation with each of them.

Chapter 20

TWO WEEKS LATER, AIMEE BLURRILY AWOKE AND found her head nestled on Gavin's chest hearing his steady heartbeat in one ear and in the other, "Please buckle your seat belts. Put up your tray tables and seat backs. We will be landing at Bangalore International Airport in twenty minutes." The crisp voice of the stewardess crackled through the first class cabin.

Gavin smiled mischievously at Aimee's astonishment at finding herself leaning so intimately on him.

"I'm so sorry," stammered Aimee.

"Well, I am not," Gavin softly answered.

"Have you been able to sleep at all?"

"Yes, very well, I might add." The smile continued to spread across Gavin's handsome face.

During this first time traveling in the first class section, Aimee realized how much more comfortable she had been than she had expected, especially on such a long flight. Even so, she desperately wanted to deplane.

Ahmed, Ayesha and Connor who were in other seats in

the same cabin area were rousing themselves as well. Connor called out, "Everyone ready for India?"

Everyone, including other passengers in the vicinity, gave a hearty, "Yes!"

Awestruck, Aimee stepped dreamily from their cab as it pulled up in front of a palatial building that would be their home for the next few weeks. She observed with wonder, "So, this is the luxury hotel, The Leela Palace, in Bangalore."

To Aimee it felt more like a royal palace than a hotel. The lobby was truly magnificent with highly polished floors, priceless furnishings, and many gracefully arched doorways and openings leading into expansive gardens. Aimee had never been in a place like this before.

When Aimee entered her room, she continued to be amazed at the elegance and royal resplendence of everything. The size of her accommodations seemed as large as her entire apartment. Traveling with Gavin and company was proving to be a real treat for her. Of course, with the technological industries centered in Bangalore, all the rooms were equipped with the latest and greatest of those aspects as well, including large screen high-def televisions, a few computers, wireless connections, programmable lighting, surround sound, and other gadgets that Aimee was unfamiliar with.

Aimee was on her own for the next few hours and wanted to unpack, relax and rest. Gavin and Ahmed had some business to attend to for the afternoon and then they would join Aimee and Ayesha along with a few business associates for dinner in the hotel at the Jamavar restaurant, specializing in delectable Indian cuisine. Aimee had noticed with much excitement that there was also a pan-Asian restaurant, the Zen, located in the hotel that she planned to try when she was on her own.

That night they enjoyed a relaxing, aromatic, and scrumptious feast of delicate curry and flavorful Biryani dishes. Aimee experienced true national cuisine for the first time, knowing she wanted to do so often while she was here. The lull of the soft classical Indian music and warm food in her tummy relaxed Aimee to the point of doziness. Before she fell asleep at the table, she excused herself telling everyone that travel weariness had caught up with her. The others stayed to continue eating and meeting.

The first week passed quickly as Aimee sampled her way through the incredible culinary cuisines all around her. She had eaten at the Zen restaurant in the hotel a number of times sampling her first Korean barbecue, tasting Thai noodles, and indulging in some of her favorite dim sum and sushi lunches.

Most often with Ayesha as guide, she had visited a few fascinating historic sites, museums, and parks on her Bangalore list. Aimee also met a few members of Ayesha and Ahmed's families and shared some fun adventures going shopping and eating authentic everyday meals with them.

Aimee felt right at home and happy at the wonders of this adventure. There were only a few times that Gavin was able to join them. Though he was only available a limited amount, he was completely attentive whenever he could be with Aimee. And, she found with effort she could maintain a causal friendship with him.

At the start of the second week in Bangalore, Aimee and Ayesha attended a gathering of top executives of HolTech (an acronym for Holbrook Technologies), the largest of Holbrook's innovative companies specializing in technology and software.

Ahmed had arranged a typical style meeting of the Holbrook men for Connor, Gavin and himself with some of the key leaders in the firm on a cricket field in Bangalore.

The natives, men and women alike, including Ahmed and Ayesha, had all been raised on watching and playing cricket. Even though Connor and Gavin had been introduced to the sport on earlier trips, they were still neophytes to the game.

The people who were avid cricket enthusiasts really knew how to bat and bowl well. Unfamiliarity with the sport left Aimee watching with bemused interest and cheering enthusiastically for both teams at the same time.

As Aimee had experienced previously, these types of meetings contained a lot of physical exertion, friendly banter and business going on simultaneously. Aimee was amazed that anyone could concentrate.

She had finally determined that Gavin, Ahmed, and Connor, must have some form of auditory or photographic memories (aspects of an eidetic memory). And, this time she saw others at HolTech having the same uncanny ability of remembering numerous business details discussed during a highly competitive cricket match.

Later that evening while they were all eating dinner together, Gavin had talked to Aimee about assisting the marketing executive at HolTech with some of their advertising and design needs. Aimee agreed to help out. When it dawned on Aimee what she had done, she turned away from Gavin and complained, "Ahmed, what have I gotten myself into? How did Gavin talk me into this? Can I really do this? Am I good enough to really help their company?"

Ahmed affirmed, "Aimee, you can do this. You are totally capable. Gavin and I are both convinced this will make for a long term business collaboration.

"Tomorrow, I will accompany you to meet Jaipreet at the HolTech plant, where we are hoping you will be able to assist them, at least part time, over the next couple of weeks."

The next day Aimee found herself on a tour by small motorized vehicle of the enormous modern factory, research areas and offices of HolTech. Jaipreet, the director of marketing, beamed with sincere pride at showing Aimee around the impressive facilities. He spoke fluent English so their communication flowed smoothly, and Aimee quickly succumbed to the friendly, easy going manner of this young company executive.

Jaipreet knew his business thoroughly and kept Aimee on her toes with fresh ideas and probing questions. HolTech was making inroads into high level innovations and Aimee was thrilled to be part of seeing them being developed with soon to be launched prototypes.

Aimee felt like she was expanding her horizons and being challenged to stretch her creativity. She and Jaipreet worked together productively and harmoniously. Jaipreet fascinated Aimee with his life stories, providing her first introduction into the world being a Sikh and about Sikhism and their founder, Guru Nanak. They accomplished a great deal in their short time together and would continue their work together long distance via phone and digitally.

During the next few weeks, squeezed in between Aimee's now busy work schedule, Ayesha had taken her to a few more of the incredible places to visit on Aimee's list — sacred temples, historic landmarks, and exquisite gardens. The Lal Bagh, a botanical garden that boasted over a thousand species of flora and trees over a hundred years old was one of Aimee's favorites. All over the district, sensational gardens, lakes and parks and grand architecture had enthralled Aimee.

She had marveled at the sight of cows around the city — cows, considered sacred, were free to roam virtually anywhere. Everywhere they traveled was crowded with people. Aimee learned to be able to meander among them and to actually have a little fun watching the ever changing kaleidoscope of humanity around her.

She wandered with fascination through street markets during a Hindu festival and joined in giving Sanskrit mantras and dancing in the streets. Aimee had purchased a small Ganesha statue, a Hindu deity who helps people overcome obstacles and achieve success. She easily tucked it into her jacket pocket for safe keeping.

For the next four days, they traveled around Bhoodhan Pochampally, the Silk City where Aimee accompanied Connor, Ahmed, Ayesha and Gavin to visit families and generations of artisans, weavers and dyers. They produced superior quality cloth, intricate fabric designs, and many styles of Indian garments. Holbrook Enterprises owned a facility in the outskirts and fostered associations with a wide number of the local artisans. Aimee found the people and the entire visit extraordinary.

Now, coming into the area of the Silk City, Aimee found her awareness of people, individually and en masse, became much more sensitive and understanding. People she met here seemed sincerely grateful for what they had — and not so focused on what they might not have.

One memorable visit was made by all to one of the companies that they had created in a poverty stricken area. Holbrook Enterprises had refurbished a dilapidated building into a facility for creating finished garments from the fine silks and cottons of master weavers. The section dedicated to weaving housed a few operational looms that were over a hundred years old.

There were a handful of master weavers who had the dexterity and craftsmanship to create the unsurpassed silk and cotton cloth using these prized looms. An important part of this facility and its location was rooted in their apprenticeship programs to hire from the local community and train the next generation of master weavers and garment makers.

The surrounding areas were crammed to overflowing with ramshackle structures, none were real buildings or even adequate shelter, that appeared to recently be in the process of being fixed up. An elderly man and woman were sitting outside a small structure made of left over cardboard, wood and other cast off materials that looked like a good wind would collapse the place.

As Ahmed, Connor and Gavin strolled by, the couple rose and greeted them, "Dost (Friend), thank you. For the first time, we have clean running water and efficient sewage removal in our home and a covering on the floor. Next, we are to be getting walls and a roof. How can we thank you?" Ayesha and Ahmed spoke with them in their native dialect for a few minutes while Gavin and Connor looked on with tender regard at the grateful pair.

Ayesha later explained to Aimee how this was where some of the poorest of the poor had been living without clean water and with open sewers. Steadily, the business had been hiring these people as well as providing improvements to the living spaces. The plan was that soon all of the people here would be housed in sturdy, clean places.

The high density of people in the area necessitated compact apartments and structures that would be more like small huts, however, this would be the first time many of them would have a real and more permanent place to live. They were opposed to erecting concrete monoliths, so only small and simple, manageable places would replace the hovels.

The Holbrook men were trying to assist them in natural ways, making this a community effort rather than a mere business. Those people directly benefiting from having these highly desirable jobs and such wonderful improvements in their lives had banded together to continue helping each other and in turn to be able to reach out and help others.

Aimee asked Ayesha about what looked to her to be small

areas where gardens were being started next to the building. Ayesha lit up, "Yes, the goal is to help these people care for themselves at least in ways such as being able to grow a little food they can eat however meager it may be."

"Oh, I would love to be able to look at the gardens and see if I can help in any way. I love growing fresh vegetables, herbs, grains and fruit whenever possible as well as flowers, trees and bushes." Aimee shared with enthusiasm.

While Ahmed, Connor and Gavin went ahead to the factory to conduct their business, Ayesha accompanied a thoughtful and happy Aimee around the areas nearby and through the designated garden plots. She saw how they had easy access to plenty of water and fertilizer from cow dung.

Aimee offered a few suggestions to some of the people tending the gardens that Ayesha translated for her. Aimee received a number of toothless grins that softened the dark weather-beaten faces around her. She received wide smiles from children who were nearby either helping or simply playing in the dirt. Aimee could see that the location of the gardens, the sunshine, water, nourishment and the loving care of the people in this large community would give them ongoing successful harvests.

A young girl, a bit thin from years of insufficient nutrition, had followed Aimee around the gardens watching her every move. Aimee had shown her how to tend some of the young shoots. She had also shared a succulent orange natively grown by a few trees near the factory. The dazzling smile and hug Aimee received from the girl a few hours later had brought tears to Aimee's eyes.

That night when Ahmed, Ayesha, Connor, Gavin and Aimee were back at their hotel having dinner, Aimee shared, "I've seen and learned so much coming here. I am overflowing with new ideas. I love the people I've met, and am moved to tears at their gracious gentleness and simple humility. Thank you for bringing me with you here to India."

Chapter 21

AFTER SIX WEEKS IN BANGALORE AND OTHER surrounding southern India areas, they flew to Delhi for their next stay of two and a half months in the Delhi district and northern regions of India. As had already been arranged on their itinerary, they would spend most of the time in the capital city of New Delhi with trips to Agra, Darjeeling and the Sikkim region.

The wedding they would attend was the last week of their stay in India. Anticipation of going to see more of the various regions of India gave Aimee pause as she contemplated the vast territory and varied landscapes of India as a country and the large population of over a billion people.

The entire Delhi district was heavily populated and bustled with activity around the clock. She spent many days at the University where the Holbrook executives were deep in meetings with renowned chemists, engineers and other researchers who were assisting them with a range of new products and community development projects. Ayesha was visiting friends in the area. Aimee enjoyed roaming around the university and spending time in the campus library.

During this second month of being in India, Aimee started feeling as though she was a bit more familiar with some of the culture of India. She felt an acute affinity to the people and many of the deities and ceremonies that were an integral part of the Indian culture and history. Aimee felt as comfortable when she visited Hindu and Sikh ashrams, Muslim mosques and Buddhist temples as she was in the familiar Catholic and Christian churches.

She discovered that historically India was considered one of the oldest living civilizations with recorded history dating back over five thousand years, from the time of the Vedas. To her that implied some of the roots of many traditions and practices across modern day India had been around for millennia. Aimee realized that meant the North American cultures, including centuries of Native American traditions, were relatively young.

The day arrived for Ayesha and Aimee's outing to Agra. Aimee was thoroughly enchanted by the idea of the Taj Mahal as a memorial to love and a monument built for the sake of love. Excitement woke Aimee early, and she had plenty of time to prepare herself and pack her overnight bag before heading to breakfast.

When Ayesha came in with Ahmed, Aimee saw that she was very upset. Ayesha broke the unwelcome news that she could not go with Aimee as she had just found out about an unexpected family emergency. Aimee's disappointment was plain. Ahmed had already set an alternative plan in motion to try and salvage the trip, knowing that they could not let Aimee go alone.

A short time later, Gavin joined Aimee at the breakfast table with a small carrying case. "Aimee, we have arranged for me to take you to Agra. Our cab is out front. We need to leave now as our train leaves soon."

Aimee was momentarily taken aback. Because of her focused desire to go on this trip, she obediently followed Gavin to an awaiting cab. Incredulous that she now found herself alone with Gavin, traveling to a place dedicated to love un-nerved her.

They caught a morning train in New Dehli and arrived a little more than three hours later in Agra. Gavin took Aimee to the hotel where they had an overnight reservation and enjoyed a refreshing lunch. Gavin's kind and gallant behavior soothed her, and she relaxed in spite of the mystifying circumstances.

Their visit to the Taj Mahal proved a profound experience. Aimee marveled at the grandeur and the intricate details of this superb masterpiece with its unsurpassed architectural beauty. The love story that inspired the creation of this spectacular memorial, this eighth wonder of the world, captivated her imagination.

Predominantly of white marble with its pearly surface, this complex of structures gleamed brightly in the afternoon sun. When Aimee entered the main chamber and looked up at the incredible domed ceiling with its exquisitely decorated arches, her eyes had grown wide open with amazement.

Everywhere they went, she was in awe. She had never been to a place like this before.

Throughout the buildings and landscape, intricate and colorful ornamentation of mosaics, glazed tiling, inlays, carving, stucco and paintings radiated care and artistry as a tribute to a love that was tangible to Aimee. The artist in Aimee admired the skilled use of color, materials and precious gems — jasper, jade, crystal, turquoise, sapphire, lapis lazuli, amethyst, onyx, coral, and carnelian — found throughout.

Over the last couple of months, Gavin had noticed how they both had been busy and that time together had been minimal. Gavin had a compelling desire to keep in physical and tangible touch with Aimee. Gavin tenderly and gently held her hand and rested his hand upon her arm or shoulder or her back. Aimee was so dazzled walking through this masterpiece of art and architecture that she hardly noticed his touch.

After touring the entire Taj Mahal, Aimee felt as though she was floating in a heaven world. This feeling continued into the evening as Gavin and Aimee stayed for the sunset, a time considered as one of the best times to see spectacular glory of the mausoleum. Gavin could feel his heart full of the love emanating from the holy grounds flowing through him to Aimee. When they were standing by the pools in front of the main entrance, he leaned her back into his solid frame.

Their heartbeats and breath began to synchronize together in mutual reverence and awe at the holy and unparalleled beauty of their surroundings. The spectacular rose glow of the entire Taj Mahal and the reflections in the pools were breathtaking. They were both aglow from the experience and even

Aimee felt herself growing deeply bonded with Gavin at having experienced these precious moments together.

Before they were scheduled to leave and return to their hotel for the night, Gavin turned Aimee to him and held her in his tender embrace. In the darkening night, he smiled at her so brightly that Aimee averted her eyes, "Aimee, do you know how much I care for you?"

Aimee's internal thoughts were a bit jumbled. Wondering if he was going to kiss her, Aimee half-heartedly turned. A conflict warred inside of her because she wanted to feel his soft lips kissing her — and at the same time she did not. In her own mind she maintained that she was not the one for him. She reminded herself that she wanted to focus on creating her own company and not becoming involved with her chief client.

She breathed out a despairing sigh, "Oh, Gavin..." as she stepped away from his embrace, immediately missing his warmth.

•••••❀•••••

The next morning Gavin had an additional surprise for Aimee. He wanted to take her a short distance to Sikandra to visit Akbar's tomb. The fifteenth-century mughal emperor, Akbar, was well known for his many and widely varied achievements in art, culture, architecture, politics, and philosophy and religion. The history and serenity of the area was awe inspiring. Aimee experienced a deep reverence at being able to walk where Akbar had walked.

That afternoon they made their return trip in their own quiet contemplation. Aimee knew she had been transformed in some way. She was not yet able to articulate what had happened to her, only that she knew something deeply mystical had taken place, and even though she did not want to admit it, Gavin was a contributor to what was changing deep inside of her.

Chapter 22

BACK IN NEW DEHLI, CONNOR AND AHMED BROUGHT Gavin up to date on what had transpired while he had gone to Agra. Aimee had a call from Jaipreet who asked if she could create a logo for one of their new products. By the next day, they had settled back into a routine of their scheduled work and activities.

Like the first part of their India journey, the second part was going very quickly. It was now the last month of their India journey, and two nights before Gavin, Connor and Aimee were scheduled to travel to the Darjeeling and Sikkim regions, Aimee decided to wander in the lush gardens around the hotel. The New Dehli night warm and clear, Aimee knew Gavin and the others were attending to business.

After an hour of walking in the peaceful well-groomed gardens, she found herself back inside the hotel near the restaurant where the Holbrook men were now conducting business over dinner. She was contemplating what she might do about dinner for herself when without warning, a woman stealthily moved to her side and spoke distinctly in her ear as though telling a secret and asked, "Are you looking for Mr. Holbrook?" There was a slight accent to her words that may have been familiar, however, Aimee was unable to pinpoint it at that moment.

"No, are you? How do you know him?"

As Aimee turned to look over this woman, she saw a stunning Indian beauty who was fashionably dressed. Her red silk, floor-length dress was low cut at the bodice and clung to her luscious curves. She was openly stroking an elaborate necklace of sparkling diamonds and red rubies that were in the style of a famous jewelry designer. Aimee looked up to stare into the iciest dark eyes she had ever seen before.

"Ah Gavin, he is my love, my paramour. You know what a paramour is, do you not? I am meeting him here for dinner." It seemed to Aimee that there had been a distinct purring sound of triumph to her voice as she had spoken these heart stabbing words. And then, with a great whisper as though this was a naughty secret and a seductive laugh, this vixen added "and a little time alone together afterward."

With sufficient pause to ensure that Aimee had received the full impact of her message, the beauty maliciously continued, "Gavin had mentioned an American woman was coming with him to work. Seeing you, I presume you are the one. Aimee is it? I am Yreesha. So very nice to meet you."

She brandished a yellowed newspaper photo and taunted, "Have you seen this?" Through a blur of tears, Aimee could see this lush beauty intimately draped over the broad shouldered body of a man who looked just like Gavin.

If Aimee had hold of her senses, she would have seen the evil gleam in Yreesha's eyes. Instead her vision had clouded with tears and her thoughts preoccupied with doubt. Aimee turned and stumbled away. She also heard an ugly sound of shrill laughter.

"No," she cried with heartbreaking anguish. If Aimee had allowed herself a moment to listen carefully, she might have considered the wee small voice of her own heart telling her the truth.

Feet frozen to the ground, Aimee had watched through the front window as Yreesha had entered the restaurant and headed over to Gavin, who had just risen to shake hands with the others. It looked like they had just finished with business. Yreesha put a hand on Gavin's shoulder. Aimee saw him give Yreesha a nod of recognition.

Not being able to stand any more, Aimee fled back to her hotel room with her emotions in shambles. She could not remember how she got into her room — only that she had tried to arrive before her composure totally disintegrated but found she had already been sobbing as she jammed the digital key in the lock. She burned with shame and anger over her circumstances.

Aimee had felt that Gavin and she were starting to share the beginnings of caring for each other. She had just begun to allow herself to acknowledge that she might be falling in love with him, and now she must face what she discovered was his betrayal at having a mistress. In her unsteady, emotionally distraught state her thoughts exaggerated the situation into an overwrought misbelief that Gavin might have many lovers in cities around the world.

"I must confront him, of course." Aimee spoke to herself half-heartedly. "He must explain. Oh, what if he lies to me. What am I to do?" At the protest of her own inner voice, Aimee decided to close her heart to further pain and hurt and to shut Gavin out.

Aimee avoided Gavin the next day by feigning a headache. That evening when he went to check on her, she refused the answer the door and pretended to be asleep.

That night Connor asked Gavin, "What's going on between you and Aimee? There seems to be some serious tension in the air."

Gavin shrugged, frustration lacing his response, "She seems to be angry with me and yet will not tell me what it is. I have no idea. What am I to do?"

Connor could only suggest, "Try to ask her. Be patient with her. She's been going through a lot that's new to her on this trip. Aimee is an amazing woman. I believe you two are well suited if you can both get through your stubbornness."

"You mean her stubbornness."

Heartily laughing, Connor sputtered, "Oh, of course, only she's stubborn."

Chapter 23

IN THE MORNING AIMEE TOOK GREAT CARE TO COVER the dark circles under her eyes and to brush color on her now pale cheeks caused by two sleepless nights. When she met Gavin at breakfast, she averted her face and spent time concentrating on speaking with Ayesha. Near the end of the meal, Aimee glanced surreptitiously at Gavin through lowered lashes and witnessed his look of hurt and his overall sad looking countenance.

They flew into Bagdogra and then traveled the rest of the way to Darjeeling by taxi. While traveling, Aimee remembered the book she had read about Mother Teresa's train ride to Darjeeling when she had received her call to live among and work with the poor and to leave the confines of the convent. And, what a life altering event that was for Mother Teresa. Aimee paused to wonder what her call might be.

A distressed atmosphere surrounded Aimee. She avoided looking at Gavin and kept her distance, avoiding any close proximity to him. Gavin looked quizzically at Aimee, trying to discern what happened to cause her to close herself off from him.

Upon arriving in Darjeeling, Aimee felt like this was her true home and that her feet had walked this land before. The view of the Himalayan mountains was spectacular.

Kanchenjunga, the third highest peak of the entire range, clearly stood out as a tall sentinel, reminding her of a wonderful painting of this vista by Nicholas Roerich. Aimee later learned that Mount Everest, the tallest peak in the Himalayas, was also the tallest mountain on earth. Along with K2, the second highest, neither was visible from Darjeeling.

A momentary glimpse of Khan's retreat came to mind, though Aimee understood she might not find it in physical form, she felt the strong pull of its presence nearby.

Aimee could also sense the presence of her friend, Tenzing. He had shared some of his stories of growing up in the foothills of the Himalayas in refugee camps of Tibetans who had been forced to flee their native homelands. Tenzing had also shared highlights of his colorful culture and some of his Tibetan Buddhism traditions.

Her feet continued to lead her to walk along well worn pathways. Aimee experienced a growing sense of familiarity with this Himalayan region. "Was I here before? Have I lived here before?"

Aimee's own thoughts surprised her. She shook her head to try and clear it. Having been raised in the Catholic faith, her past Christian upbringing did not give her any previous experience of knowing about reincarnation. Yet before her was a clear vision of time spent in this sacred land.

Since visiting India, she no longer believed in exclusivity toward one set of devotions or beliefs. She now embraced a more universal and global attitude and applauded every sincere form of devotion. Her entire soul was free to embrace mystical beliefs held both in the east and the west, and she found happiness in this freedom.

Though feeling a bit torn in her unresolved state about her perceived deceit on Gavin's part, Aimee could not hold back her enthusiasm at being in Darjeeling and sharing what she was experiencing with Gavin and the others. Aimee still maintained her physical distance from Gavin though she shared some of her wondrous stories with him while others were around.

Gavin tried to ask Aimee about what was going on, but she skirted the subject and kept herself from being alone with him. He did not understand Aimee's continuing coldness toward him, and he questioned what his heart had been telling him.

The next two days Connor and Gavin were scheduled to take Aimee on a short excursion into the Sikkim region to tour a few of the villages and some of the area not far from Darjeeling. He was determined to discover what was going on with Aimee.

However, the morning they were to leave, Connor decided he needed to stay in Darjeeling to work with one of their associates, and, unknown to Gavin and Aimee, to be there when John arrived. John had called Connor the previous night to announce he would be arriving midday, as Jagadayu had convinced him to come to India for his wedding to Trilochana.

Jagadayu and John had work intensely together a few years earlier, and Jagadayu continued to claim that his ongoing success was a result of John's expert guidance.

John decided since he was flying to India, he would come a few days before the wedding to meet up with Connor, Gavin and Aimee in Darjeeling, and then return to Delhi with them for the wedding celebrations.

John, the most adventurous of the Holbrook men, loved the Darjeeling region and when possible came to participate in escorted treks into the Himalayas. This time he would not have the luxury of going on any such hikes. Instead, he planned to visit one of his favorite gardens to gather fresh Darjeeling tea to take home to his wife.

That morning neither man knew of the incredible serendipitous importance of the presence of both of them in Darjeeling that afternoon.

Chapter 24

GAVIN AND AIMEE HAD HEADED INTO THE SIKKIM region with a tour service in a jeep on a commonly used, seat sharing basis. Aimee had taken the front seat, leaving Gavin to sit with two other tour members. At points in the journey there were misty views of the magnificent vistas of the Himalayas. They had stopped briefly at a place to see colorful butterflies and unique vegetation.

Gavin had wanted to share with Aimee some of the beauty and unique biodiversity of this special area. Though considered the least populous state and far from the more populated areas of India, more than a half a million people resided here.

After a few hours touring by jeep, Aimee was glad that they were stopping in a small town to look around, do a little shopping and get something to eat and drink. She jumped out of the vehicle and had gone ahead of Gavin.

The tour participants had been ambling through an open market in the downtown area for only a short time, when the ground began to heave and shake. Suddenly, coverings, roofs and walls were collapsing all around. Merchandise was being hurled everywhere as if everyone was the object of an enormous unwelcome food fight.

Gavin had tried to reach Aimee, who had been a few hundred feet ahead of him in the market area. She was being swept even further away from him as people crowded the street running in many different directions. Gavin saw a brief glimpse of the horror and fright on Aimee's face as she turned to look for him and was swept away by a fast moving small crush of panic stricken people.

Aimee had never felt such intense fear as what was currently moving through the press of so many sweat-laced bodies. She prayed she could stay upright for to fall would be an instant trampled death and heard herself cry in despair, "Gavin, where are you?"

After the first main tremor came the aftershocks which brought even more unrelenting panic. She could hear as people were hit by flying debris or being buried. Children were sobbing and disoriented by the loss of family and the shock of disaster. Soon there was a thinning of the crowd as they had come to a more open area just north of the town. On a small hill overlooking part of the town, Aimee found a pile of rubble rock to sit on and try to catch her breath and her wits. What she saw before her upset her deeply.

Much of the town seemed to have been violently shaken into piles of rubble. People were everywhere wandering in a daze, a few had already started to help others and tend to the wounded. Another stalwart group scavenged through the wreckage and found water and food that they brought to a central location near where Aimee sat. More and more people were soon joining in to help with the rescue efforts. Aimee got up and went to aid a mother who with her three small children were digging around trying to find their things in the rubble that had been their home.

Fortunately, they found cookware, some food items, and blankets and things which would help care for themselves and others during the days ahead. The tear-faced young woman conveyed to Aimee how her husband had been at the bazaar as a vendor, and she was worried about him. Aimee had the same worry about Gavin.

Covered in dust and mud, Aimee continued working alongside the villagers unable to tell for how long or how she would survive the coming evening and night out in the open with the rest of the town. She had never been in an earthquake and had never witnessed such destruction in just minutes. She kept busy helping others, though what she really wanted to do was find Gavin.

A young child clung to her asking for help. He had lost his entire family. She understood he had been playing in a now-nonexistent street. He dragged Aimee to where he last remembered his home was. A lot of people were in that area. Moments later a small group of people parted, and Aimee's young charge heard his name and ran into the open arms of his mother. Joy shone on both of their faces, and Aimee felt a surge of thanksgiving.

After taking a dusty breath, Aimee decided she must decide how to find Gavin. She knew she must be several miles from where they had been together. Because she had been spun around in the crowd, she was uncertain which exact direction she needed to go. She questioned her every thought and move, "And, what if he had headed the opposite or another alternate direction?"

Choking back hysterical sobs, waves of panic washed through her. She struggled with her thoughts that Khan had not appeared, warned her or shown her other opportunities to guide her away from this disaster. In her internal anguish, she cried out, "My Khan, why of all times have you not come? Have you forsaken me? I feel so terribly frightened and so cut off from you. There are so many people hurt who I wish I could help. Where is Gavin? What of Gavin? Is he still alive? Or…?"

Aimee would not allow herself to think the worst. She wanted to pray. She stood still and began calling to every master, saint and sage and gave every form of prayer she could remember. Most fervently she asked Khan for his help. She was certain assistance was needed from every possible source for her to find Gavin and for them to get back to Darjeeling and Connor.

Aftershocks continued to shake the region as Aimee stumbled forward in the direction she was compelled to go. Periodically, she bowed her head and implored, "Khan, help these people and help me find Gavin alive."

Speaking her doubts and asking for Khan's help, strengthened her. She was resolute to continue in her quest to find Gavin. Aimee felt assured that it was her destiny to have come here. In the back of her mind a memory tugged at her about weathering disasters and helping and praying for others. Little bits and pieces of Khan talking with her over the years came to her mind. He had asked her to keep an ongoing vigil with him and to pray for the earth and the people around the world. He had foreseen much planetary upheaval and turbulence.

Aimee began to recognize how Khan had helped guide her to choose to come to India, to be here during this disaster, and to help in both inner and outer ways, continuing to aid him in his overall purposes. She knew she had to find Gavin and that her future was intricately entwined with his.

Unable to bear the thought that Gavin might be seriously injured, Aimee raced forward toward what was left of the main area of town. In the recesses of Aimee's mind and heart, she pondered why it took a disaster for her to recognize the depth of her feelings for this wonderful man.

"Oh Gavin, please forgive me." Aimee spoke out loud as though to force the air to carry her message to Gavin, wherever he might be.

"Why couldn't I have accepted that you truly cared for me as you tried repeatedly to tell me? And, why has it taken me until now to realize how much I care for you?" The question throbbed through her thoughts.

Aimee kept moving for the next few hours as the sun began to set. She stopped frequently to help someone with moving rubble and to search for others, food and necessary belongings. When she stopped to assist a man dig out a small child who had been entombed in a protective cave of fallen concrete and timber, Aimee felt a flicker of hope that she would find Gavin alive.

After this successful rescue, Aimee again stumbled on. Her legs were exhausted and no longer steady. She badly wanted to drop to the ground where she was and go no further. She realized that she had grown exceedingly thirsty and hungry, yet she went on, compelled to unrelentingly persevere as though being led on a rope to find Gavin. She pictured his warm, loving smile. And regretfully, remembered how her rejection had caused him sadness and confusion.

The dark was encroaching more and more quickly around her. There were a few candles glowing in the dark, however, without electricity or gas, there was insufficient illumination by which to see, and with a cloud covered sky, the night would be black.

She had just about given up hope in her utterly exhausted despair. Fully spent and ready to collapse, Aimee was weaving across an area strewn with many piles of rubble and debris. Somehow, she kept forging ahead a little further, way beyond the limit of her endurance.

A little cry erupted from Aimee's throat as she stumbled over what looked in the shadows as a large body. A deep long moan came from the area of her feet. The sound awakened a deep inner recognition within her.

"Gavin?..."

A small croaking sound that seemed to say, "Aimee?" emerged from the body laying motionless on the ground at her feet.

"Gavin, is it really you? Can you move?" In the grey light Aimee could not tell for certain it was Gavin, yet she knew it was him. She touched him to embrace him and had to withdraw as he cried out loudly, pain evident in the sound.

Later, she would weep with gratitude at having found him

and to realize that if she had quit when she thought she was at her end, she would have missed him.

"Badly hurt...can't get up...knocked out...people helped unbury..." Gavin strained to keep speaking as his voice became weaker and his words less coherent. Soon Gavin drifted into unconsciousness.

With as much calm and energy as Aimee could muster, she whispered to Gavin, "Stay still. We will rest here for the night." Aimee was already lightly touching him to see if she could tell if there were any open wounds or broken bones. She quavered with dry tears. She did not have enough moisture to shed the rivers of sorrow she felt.

Even in her exhaustion, she softly crooned and hummed to relax and comfort him. She choked out, "Hang on. In the morning I will get help. Gavin, please don't leave me. " Aimee silently prayed that he could feel the energy of her heart enwrapping him to help keep him alive.

Aimee gently nestled next to Gavin to try and keep him warm. The dark night was difficult as the uneven ground and hard rubble bruised both of them even more than they already were. Gavin's moans woke Aimee throughout the night. She tried to ease his agony with little success. She knew he must need water and nourishment soon as she herself needed them as well.

In the haze of her exhaustion, Aimee was aroused with a start as the sun was fully shining. She admonished herself for having fallen asleep. She had wanted to get help at first light. She heard a loud groan and realized it was her sounding out the pain of her stiff muscles. She anguished over what she could now see was shredded and bloody remnants of what had been his clothes.

Countless darkening bruises and small scratches covered his body. He had a large lump and gash on his head and badly skinned and scratched palms and knees that looked like he must have tried to crawl. He was completely covered in dust mingled with blood.

Aimee knew she had to get immediate help. She figured it must be nearly twenty-four hours since the first jolting quake. "Gavin, stay here. I'm going to find water and food for us and get help for you."

She valiantly tried to cover as much exposed skin as possible to keep him from getting sunburned. Aimee carefully studied the location of where Gavin lay so that she could get back to him. Then, without further delay, she headed to an area that looked to be less than a mile away where she could see some people had gathered. She hoped they had water and food and could maybe provide some medical assistance. Sheer determination kept her trudging forward as she shook and swayed uncontrollably.

Even walking that relatively short distance, Aimee's uneven gait slowed her down. After what seemed an excruciatingly long time, Aimee finally arrived where people had created a make shift emergency center with limited amounts of water, food and supplies.

She was able to drink a little water and ate a small bit of fruit. She found a few bandages and a very small amount of antiseptic. She gathered water and food to take to Gavin. As she was weaving through debris in what once were streets, someone stopped her with a strong handhold on her arm.

"Aimee, is that you?"

Unaware of her own dust covered, tattered appearance, Aimee wondered how anyone who knew her might have to ask. The voice seemed like one she should know. Dully, she looked over to see lightly dusted pants.

As her weary eyes looked up to find the face, a flicker of recognition glinted in her eyes and she exclaimed, "Connor! Thank God."

Then, all awareness escaped her as she collapsed into him in a complete faint.

Bewildered, Aimee opened her eyes to see Connor bent over her dripping water onto her lips and heard him gently calling her name. Aimee could not fathom why she was on the ground. She kept struggling to tell Connor, "… must get Gavin." It took several minutes for Connor to fully understand her raspy sounds.

"Do you know where Gavin is? Is he alive? Is he hurt?" Hope was apparent in Connor's shaky voice.

Connor carefully and patiently administered water and a little juice to try and strengthen her. When she could stand and plod along by leaning upon him, Connor called over to someone nearby who was gathering some supplies. She had been aware that there was at least one other person hovering about and had not had the strength to discern who exactly it was or to greet them.

She heard Connor say something about making a chair for her and then thought John was talking. "How could John be here?" She felt so fuzzy. She wanted to find Gavin.

"Now can you lead us to Gavin?" The familiar voice of John urged. Connor and John had created a little hammock type seat between them so she could sit and lean on both of them while they carried her. Still incredibly weak, they hoisted Aimee up. She could only nod and point in the direction they needed to go.

Fortunately, Connor and John were strong. Even in their fine athletic shape, it took an arduous hour for them to locate Gavin. They had rested a few times and had stopped to give a much needed helping hand.

When they finally found Gavin, he was where Aimee had left him and was still unresponsive. Connor and John worked quickly to examine him. John frowned and looked worried.

He knew enough wilderness emergency first aid to recognize the severity of Gavin's condition and to be concerned about Aimee as well. Gavin was unable to fully gain consciousness though he hovered near it. Aimee had instantly fallen into an exhausted slumber when they had set her down near Gavin's prone body.

John voiced what they both knew, "We have to find a way to get Gavin and Aimee to a hospital immediately."

Chapter 25

IT HAD TAKEN A TREMENDOUS RESCUE EFFORT AND into the late evening before Gavin and Aimee were airlifted by helicopter from the earthquake stricken area to a hospital in Darjeeling. Though the distance was not far, road travel had been disrupted. The quick and efficient mobilization of the Indian rescue teams had been what saved the day. Pilots had been shuttling the most grievously wounded to triage locations and hospitals within reasonable flight distance.

Several days had passed before Connor and John were able to make their way to Darjeeling themselves and get to the hospital to check on their friends. While Aimee was in a deep and restless sleep, they had heard her muttering. She had cried out in great distress, "Yreesha, you cannot have him. He is mine! All mine. Khan, Gavin is mine. All mine. She cannot have him."

Replays of disaster scenes ran through Aimee's semiconscious state and as she was awakening, she saw Gavin alive and well, laughing, holding her and looking in her eyes as only he could do — showering her with love and simultaneously drawing forth love from her. She began to reason that she no longer cared about any other women in Gavin's life. She would cherish whatever time she could have with him.

Connor was sitting by Aimee's bed when she finally awoke. She found an IV was attached to her and looked over at Connor questioningly.

"You were dehydrated so the IV is providing some much needed fluids and nutrients as well. How are you feeling?"

Throat parched, Aimee rasped, "It seems I am alive. Where's Gavin?"

"He is in critical condition and is under the care of friends of ours who are doctors and nurses caring for earthquake victims here in Darjeeling. It's been three days since the quake. They gave you a sedative to maintain a more peaceful slumber because you were so restless and seemed haunted by something."

"Oh, Connor," Aimee paused to rest her aching voice, "What have I done?"

"You have done nothing other than to be bewitched by the evil intent of Yreesha's wiles." Connor held up his hand to tell Aimee to allow him to speak and for her to listen. "John and I heard you calling her name and shouting that she could not have him and that he is yours — all yours."

Aimee gave a slight shudder as she remembered the menacing cold eyes of Yreesha. She frowned in an attempt to recall what Connor was talking about.

"You were thrashing about and repeating your words several times. John and I briefly wondered how you would come to know of Yreesha, and then we determined that she must have somehow made contact with you the day of our business meetings. You claimed a headache the next day that Gavin was puzzled about. He told us you would not see him which all of us thought seemed out of character."

Connor paused to make sure Aimee was still following him as he knew she was a little fuzzy from her drug induced sleep.

When Connor continued with confidence and soft compassion, "You had turned so aloof and cold toward all of us, especially Gavin. He was concerned that it was because you had been ill. His desire to be with you was so great that we did not cancel coming up into the mountains."

Connor cleared his throat and went on, "Eight years ago, Gavin was in New Dehli with Joseph to finalize one of our business partnerships. As they were walking on the streets of the city, Gavin spied a young woman who was wearing ragged clothing and peddling her wares, herself. Even in rags, they could all see her inherent beauty.

"His compassion took hold and he asked one of the Indian businessmen who accompanied them if they would willingly hire this woman to do work in one of their plants. The man had hesitated, but not wanting to seem uncharitable, agreed to the arrangement. Gavin also asked that she be allowed to bathe, given food, fresh water and some simple clean clothing. As you can imagine this was none other than your antagonist Yreesha.

"Gavin quickly forgot about her. The businessman had done as promised and had her working in one of his plants.

Over the next several years, Yreesha flourished. However, something seemed to snap inside of her when the young plant manager where she worked got married.

"He was a man of wealth, good looks and humor. Just the kind of man Yreesha would have wanted for herself. He had married a young woman for her kindness and loving nature — she had no wealth and was no ravishing beauty. This was an auspicious and very happy union.

"We believe Yreesha had hoped to wed this plant manager and that she could not understand his choice of his bride over her. Jealously may have temporarily corrupted her into a scheming vixen.

"Yreesha had discovered from the businessman who had initially helped her that it was really Gavin who was her benefactor. She must have decided now was the time to contact him directly. When she found out we were in Dehli meeting with business associates, she determined to make herself known.

"She wanted to make an impact and finagled Gavin into several situations where she could be publicly introduced under the illusion that she was someone he had known in an intimate way. She cunningly played the role in dress and allure."

Connor stopped and asked, "Aimee, are you feeling up to continuing with this?"

"There is much treachery by Yreesha against Gavin, and now, recently against you as well."

"Go on. She had a news photo." Aimee whispered so softly Connor barely heard her.

"Yes, the photo. Years ago Yreesha staged this camera shoot by coming to the hotel where all of us had gathered for dinner. Yressha made a grand entrance dragging along a cameraman from one of the news media stations who had come along to get a few interviews.

"Moving like a cheetah on the hunt, Yreesha stalked over to Gavin, immediately plastered herself against him and with a seductive smile told Gavin to say cheese while the camera flashed. Of course, Gavin was in such shock that only surprise showed on his face. The gossip said that it was surprise at being found with his lover."

Aimee unconsciously groaned. Connor checked to see if she was okay. Aimee gently moved her hand indicating she wished him to continue.

"Gossip prevailed for a few weeks. The paparazzi had been waiting for years to find out about Gavin's personal life and to discover his lovers and unearth any gossip in the life of this handsome, intriguing and fairy-tale–too-good-to-be-true man that the tidbits Yreesha threw out grew exponentially.

"We did our own quiet campaign and in a few months things were back to an even keel though a little damage had been done to Gavin's reputation in a few quarters, especially as Yreesha kept on with her stories in the local area.

"John and I believe she had become the mistress of some-one in the executive branch at the headquarters of the offices we partner with in Dehli and that she has been able to find out our itineraries and about Gavin's personal life. We have a good idea of who it is, though we have not been able to confirm this or to confront him. Aimee, he is a married man with a number of children, and we do not want to hurt his wife and children.

"Obviously, we did not act quickly enough before she created the scene with you and caused damage to your trust of Gavin's honor. John and I only hope it is repairable and that you meant what you said that he is yours – all yours – and in our minds, only yours."

Tears were gently falling from Aimee's closed eyes. She berated herself as she wondered why she had not trusted Gavin and asked him about this woman rather than hardening her heart to him without giving him a chance. She knew she had wallowed in self-made misery and her heart ached.

Connor touched her hand and added softly, "I know Gavin loves you. I know there is no one else. And, most importantly, I know that you are the one for him."

He continued to explain, "Yreesha will no longer bother you. There is a young man at the plant where she works who wishes to marry her. She has agreed and is now busy planning her wedding. Yreesha has been lonely and lacking in self-respect. Maybe now she can find her way with the help of the love of a caring husband."

John sat beside her as Connor spoke and took her trembling hand in comfort as Aimee slipped into the restorative sleep of those suffering from exhaustion and grievous wounds.

"You know," John mused. "Love has a strange kind of power to change the very nature of people and things — sort of like transformational alchemy."

Chapter 26

Aimee awoke to questions sounding within her, "Oh, Khan, why? Why has this all happened?"

Somewhere inside of herself, she knew the answer. In college her class had studied Shakespeare's play, *Much Ado About Nothing*, and she had prided herself in seeing through the unspeakable harm caused by the false accusations against Hero by Don John. Aimee had earned a top grade for writing about communication and open-hearted trust and caring.

Now, she clearly saw how jealousy and false pride had taught her the lesson to see truth with her heart and soul. She had been swayed by gossip and malevolence. She felt ashamed of her own thoughts and feelings in reaction to Yreesha's spiteful lies rather than relying on her own inner intuition and trusting Gavin. How quickly hurt and anger had taken over and hardened her heart against him.

And now, Gavin was valiantly hanging on to dear life, fighting for breath and consciousness.

On a particularly difficult day, while in search of a handkerchief to dry her tears, she discovered her forgotten Ganesha statue in her pocket. Aimee nestled the little statue near his pillow, prayed for Gavin to be fully healed, and envisioned Ganesha removing all obstacles to his complete and speedy recovery.

For the next week, Gavin continued to mend. Because of the severity of his head injuries, no one knew with complete certainty if he would regain all of his mental and physical capabilities. Aimee stayed by his side and slept on a narrow cot in the same room. She talked to him, encouraging him with hope, and read many uplifting and inspiring stories of courage, miraculous healings, and people beating the odds.

Gavin steadily gained in strength and in the restoration of all his faculties. He continued on a slow and steady path to healing. When it was clear he would recover, the doctors agreed that he could be released from the hospital with his promise that he would continue to take it easy for the next few weeks.

During his last night in the hospital Gavin awoke in the wee hours of the night, comforted to find Aimee sleeping on the cot nearby. The room was lit only with a small hospital light when unexpectedly an intense iridescent light illumined the entire room. Gavin saw a tall, elegantly dressed and turbaned man standing near his bed. Gavin was drawn to a pair of brilliant blue eyes piercing him with tender affection.

"Gavin, I am Khan, noble ruler of the heart. I find it is time to reveal myself to you. I have known you and Aimee for a very long time. I have been, and continue to be, a master teacher and guide to each of you. At times you have had a glimpse of my presence or my light energy. There have been moments when you sensed me nearby without knowing who I was.

"Throughout your entire life, you have received my guidance, and you have had the courage to make wise choices by following your own heart and intuition. And, I have had the privilege to watch you attain a great deal of well deserved success and happiness.

"When Aimee was twelve, during a difficult moment in her life, I desired to answer her prayers and appeared to her to offer guidance. Since then, she has continued to invite me into her life. Her tender heart is easily bruised, and she has had difficulty allowing her heart to be guided by love and love alone."

For the next twenty minutes, Khan continued to converse with Gavin and share many more things with him. At some point, Khan had gently placed his hand on Gavin's forehead. Gavin's entire body had instantly relaxed.

As time passed, Gavin could feel intense energy flowing through him, causing him a light tingling all over. The energy increased steadily until Gavin felt a deep burning in his chest, predominantly in his heart, and he saw a fiery pink glow all around him. When Khan was finished, he gently withdrew his hand and stepped back to where he had first appeared.

Khan advised, "I recommend you wait to tell Aimee the details of our meeting until she has opened herself fully to the love you offer her.

"You are welcome to talk with me at any time. Tell me any

and every thing, and ask anything of me. Call to me whenever you have need of me and know that I will continue to be with you always."

In the next instant, the Khan and the iridescent illumination were gone. Tears of joy freely flowed down Gavin's cheeks as he gave gratitude for the indescribable love he felt from Khan, and for Khan. He felt as if every cell and atom in his body was trying to absorb as much of the light and love that Khan had given him.

The next morning Aimee could sense a change in Gavin, though she could not pinpoint it. Impossible as it might be, he seemed to have more energy and a new vigor. He also appeared as though he was more radiant. She did not want to alarm Gavin by asking him about these things as she thought it might be just her imagination.

A few hours after leaving the hospital, Aimee and Gavin stood on the balcony of the Darjeeling hotel where they were staying for the night. They were both deep into their own thoughts as they looked out at the spectacular views. They had their arms entwined around each other in gladness that they were both alive. They etched into their memories the view before them of snow capped Himalayan mountain peaks sharply edged against a brilliant blue sky.

Chapter 27

THE NEXT DAY THEY TRAVELED BACK TO NEW Delhi. They were rejoining the others to attend the wedding celebrations of a pair of friends who both worked at Delhi University and for many years collaborated closely with John, Ahmed, Connor and Gavin. Lovely Trilochana, was marrying her lifelong friend and love, Jagadayu.

The celebrations were lavish and lasted for five full days. All of them were housed at a luxury home of a member of Trilochana's family along with other immediate family and a few friends of the family. This afforded Gavin a convenient place to continue to take it easy and convalesce as he had promised.

The wedding feasts were extravagant displays of food laden tables, including an abundance of delicious, vibrant vegetarian dishes. Gavin whispered that any uneaten food would not go to waste, as in some wedding ceremonies, but would be taken immediately to several places not far away where people were gathering for their own feasting and taking food back home with them.

Jagadayu and Trilochana were a splendid couple. Richly arrayed in colorful, exquisite silks and soft cottons, they looked like prince and princess. Intricate necklaces of fine gold and earrings and nose rings of elegant gold and silver, embellished with gemstones, were evident in abundance. The traditional henna art on the arms of the bride was complemented with a multitude of jangling bracelets. The visual splendor of the entire wedding, reception and celebration was superbly dazzling.

Trilochana and her friends had helped Aimee dress in the priceless silk sari Gavin had presented to her before the trip. They had also given her bracelets, anklets with tiny bells, and a simple gold necklace and earrings. Trilochana's mother had pierced Aimee's nose and given her a tiny sparkling crystal to wear as an adornment.

There was a great deal of lively and energetic music and dancing in the Bhangra style. A group of award winning Bhangra performers demonstrated the various moves and had everyone jumping in. Accompanying the dancers was the traditional dhol drum, along with a variety of string and other drum instruments.

Aimee had become completely immersed in the festivities and tried to follow the hand, feet and body movements that went with this lively Indian music. The music was fast paced and everyone joined in — laughing, singing and dancing concurrently. Aimee decided to just wave her hands in the air and move around, jump up and down, swing her feet, clap every now and then. She laughed when she noticed a few other people were doing the same.

After a few hours of this energetic dancing, Aimee was breathless and stopped to take a break. She stepped outside into the garden. Aimee felt Gavin's presence quietly shadowing her. His soft sighs preceded his gentle caressing touch. The joy of the moment caused Aimee to lean back into Gavin's strong, powerful embrace. She did not know when she had come to love Gavin. She only knew now with clarity that she truly loved him with her whole heart and soul.

Chapter 28

IMMEDIATELY AFTER THE FINAL CELEBRATIONS, JOHN was scheduled to return home. The others were flying home the next day. Outside in front of the house where they had lived and celebrated for the last five days, Connor, Ahmed and Gavin were saying their farewells as they waited with John for his ride to the airport to arrive. John had already said his goodbyes to Ayesha and Aimee inside the house.

They found that this was an emotional moment for all of them. They continued to be swamped by the enormity of what had taken place these last few weeks. They knew a power greater than all of them must have arranged this entire trip and saved Gavin's life. John continued to be astounded at how he had gone to Darjeeling, arrived there in the precise moment when he could help rescue Gavin and Aimee, and witnessed Gavin's complete recovery.

With a wobble in his voice, John hugged Gavin for a second time and added, "Buddy, thank God you are coming home with us. Though we never gave up hope, it was too close for comfort. Love you bro, safe journey home. Hawk's beside himself with wanting us home."

After John release him, Gavin cleared his throat and shared his recent thoughts, "Though I am anxious to get back home, I want to ask if it's okay with all of you if I extend my stay in India by a few more days before I return home? I'm going to see if Aimee will stay too. I feel compelled to travel back to Darjeeling and to take Aimee with me. You all are welcome to come as well or return as planned."

They stared at Gavin, and as understanding dawned, their faces lit up with genuine happiness and humor. Back slapping and replies overlapped.

"About time, Gav." "Sure. Just make sure and call us immediately with the news." "Yahoo!" "We'll leave you two alone." "Thank Krishna!"

Ahmed concluded, "The rest of us will go home tomorrow as planned, so it will be just you and Aimee."

When, as hoped, Aimee expressed her desire to stay with Gavin, Connor arranged for Gavin and Aimee to return home five days later so they could spend three full days in Darjeeling.

Before dinner when Connor, Ahmed, Ayesha, Gavin and Aimee would gather for the last time in India, only Ahmed knew that Gavin had slipped away earlier in the day on a mysterious errand to visit an old friend in New Dehli.

Being back in Darjeeling gave Aimee additional time to contemplate the significance of her entire trip to India. Aimee had learned to love the people and culture of India. She had come to know many Hindu deities including, Ganesha, Shiva, Krishna, Radha, and Lakshmi. She had discovered Sikhism, learned more about Muslim and Buddhist faiths, and been immersed in Tibetan culture.

Her heart had opened to many holy, kind, and gentle people — some possessed little in material goods and others had great wealth. She had bonded with people of all ages and all stations in life, from beggar to prince.

In the land of India, Aimee had come to an even greater awareness of the magnificence of Khan and the wonder of his presence in her life. Aimee knew that Khan was truly a tremendous holy one who was for her a most devoted loving father, teacher and guardian. He was grand master and guru in the truest sense. As Aimee sent intense gratitude and love to him, she felt the Khan draw close to her. She knew he was thanking her for recognizing and embracing him in her life. She thought, "That's the Khan for you —always loving and gracious."

On the hotel balcony and deep in meditation with Khan, Aimee was startled by Gavin speaking behind her. She had not heard him approach. "The mountains are magnificent, are they not?"

Aimee turned to Gavin, saying "Yes, I was just thinking about making this image into a piece of art for your personal love note."

Gavin chuckled, "Oh, so you know me well enough now?"

Pausing, he gazed longingly at the distant peaks, and added, "I have a secret to tell you. Somewhere in these majestic mountains is the retreat of the Khan."

"Who?.. What?..." Aimee asked breathlessly, wondering silently, "How does Gavin know about Khan?"

Gavin placed his hands on Aimee's shoulders. She was within inches of him. He gently tugged her to him and wrapped her in a warm embrace. Aimee could feel the warm heat of his body as they stood in the morning chill of their Himalayan surroundings.

They felt no cold. Aimee was drawn into the crystal clear depths of Gavin's eyes — into the very depths of his soul. Their connection to each other was so tangible that it was as though unseen arms were wrapped around both of them holding them even closer together than they already were.

Reluctantly, Gavin tore his gaze away from Aimee and glanced toward the mountains, enumerating, "Aimee, ma chérie, my love, he came to me. In the hospital, he came while you were sleeping. He told me he is known as the Khan, noble ruler of the heart. Khan said he has an ethereal retreat here in Darjeeling.

"He blessed me and said that you and I are parts of one whole. And, he acknowledged that he has been with us for many ages, and that this time, you have known him since age twelve. While he was blessing me, I felt an intense burning deep in my chest and saw an extraordinary pink glow surrounding me. I was completely awed by this experience."

Gavin lowered luscious, soft lips to cover Aimee's. Never had she known, even dreamt, of anything like this. He deepened his kiss and Aimee sighed, leaning into him even more as her body went lax. Aimee heard little chirping sounds and realized that it was her making these happy sounds.

They walked in the afternoon sun along a path of lush foliage. Gavin used his hand at Aimee's back to guide her to a stone bench near a softly bubbling fountain. Removing a small box from his pocket, Gavin opened it to reveal an exceptional blue diamond in a simple gold setting.

Taking Aimee's hand in his, he turned to her with such love and kindness in his face that she melted under his gaze. "Aimee, will you marry me?"

Aimee gasped with pure delight, putting her hand to her wildly beating heart, she tried to steady herself enough to speak.

"Oh, Gavin." She paused as tears filled her eyes, "I love you with all my heart and soul. I admit I have been frightened, my feelings for you from the very first have been so strong — so raw and exposed, such new emotions for me. I was reluctant to commit my heart to you for fear I was unworthy of you and that you could easily break it.

"During my visit with the Khan last night, I asked if he could confirm what I was now feeling in my heart. He gave me a reassuring smile and a resounding, 'Yes!'

"So, that is my answer — Yes! I will marry you, and let's make it very soon!"

Gavin was giddy with happiness. He easily slid the ring onto Aimee's finger. It was a perfect fit. He then leaned his head and brushed his lips across Aimee's cheek and lips.

She felt a little dizzy as her pulse galloped, and Gavin tried to express his feelings, "You have made me wonderfully happy, my darling! Tomorrow, we leave this enchanted place. Together, we return home with this unforgettable magic in our hearts, a gift of love that we can share with our family and friends while we plan our glorious wedding."

Epilogue

A RESPLENDENT WEDDING IT WAS. AIMEE AND GAVIN were both blissfully happy. Both of their families and closest friends had come to celebrate their marriage. Even though they had tried to keep the numbers small, the wedding guests had totaled well over two hundred.

Gavin's parents and two sisters, their husbands and his brother with his wife had all come along with a handful of Gavin's nephews and nieces. Aimee's parents and Paul were in attendance. Hawk, Ahmed, Connor, John, Kyle (Gavin's brother), and Paul had served as groomsmen partnering with Jeena, Alkisha,Liza, Gabriella, Suze and Hope who were the lovely bridesmaids. Lillian and Ayesha were in their element serving as wedding and reception coordinators.

Grandaunt Bertie escorted to her seat by Hawk wore a dazzling smile and an I-told-you-so attitude. Love richly permeated everyone everywhere during the entire wedding and reception.

Trilochana and Jagadayu along with Jaipreet and his wife

had come from India. Other close partners and associates had traveled from India, Canada, Japan, China, France, England, Scotland and several other places in Europe.

Aimee and Gavin had decided to wear exquisite, specially made silken garments made by the hands of the artisans they had visited in India.

Gavin's tunic and pants were tailored of iridescent blue, green, gold and purple silk woven together into a soft shimmering cloth. An electric blue and gold mantle created a cape. Gavin looked like a royal prince —handsome, confident, rich and elegant.

Aimee's silk sari wedding gown was one of a kind. Hand crafted with a unique pattern designed just for her wedding gown, the material was a shimmering lightweight silk, woven like fine filigree lace.

The gown was predominantly pure white with an exquisite border of blue, green, gold and purple silk that complemented Gavin's attire. Aimee had wanted to blend the bridal traditions of the elegant and colorful Indian saris and the lovely white gowns of the West. The artisans had outdone themselves. Aimee could feel the love and care that went into her beautiful gown.

The entire church had been filled with gorgeous arrangements of flowers and uplifting floral fragrances with touches of sandalwood and cedar, creating a hint of Himalayan splendors. Everything was designed as a feast for the senses — exotic and reminiscent of the budding of their romance in India leading to this celebration of their union in matrimony.

Sweet five-year-old Sasha, John's daughter, had been the flower girl and strewn a profusion of rose, peony and lily petals before the bride. She also sent a healthy dose of petals over people sitting on both sides of the central aisle causing happy laughter to bubble throughout the church.

Music rang throughout the ceremony from family church hymns to Indian music. During the reception the music varied widely and dancing ranged from ballroom, freestyle, Indian Bhangra, folk and line dancing to the simply jumping up and down for joy type of celebrating. Everyone was able to participate and thoroughly enjoy themselves. There was a lot of hooting, hollering and singing.

The cake cutting and the bouquet and garter tossings had been filled with laughter and good natured exuberance. Duke and Duchess had joined in the melee, and to much laughter, Duke had grabbed the garter just before Gavin had been able to toss it for the first time.

The bouquet had been caught by Aimee's dear friend, Liza, and the garter had landed right in the hands of the only remaining single male of the five Holbrook founders, Connor, whose face had reddened with embarrassment. Aimee and Gavin shared giddy laughter while their family and friends joked with Liza and Connor and happily paired them up together.

During the dancing, Aimee felt compelled to go out into the night darkened garden. As she stepped into a nook of fragrant lilac bushes, she immediately saw the radiant light of Khan who was standing before her smiling widely — looking a lot like a proud papa.

"Oh Khan, I am so happy. I love Gavin so very much. What a splendid wedding and reception. And, thank you again as you brought us together, did you not?" Aimee asked with a heart full of gratitude.

"No, my dear, you both found one another because you opened your hearts. Your souls yearned for each other. You and Gavin followed your own pure desire to find true love. It was up to the two of you individually to remember and re-awaken your own divine destiny. The happiness that you share can now be expanded to bless and inspire others."

With eyes that twinkled with mirth, Khan continued. "Go now and share your wedding night with your beloved and re-member to welcome the children who want to come to you. They eagerly await."

"What… What children?" Aimee stuttered to the air where Khan had been.

She hurried back into the reception area and raced swiftly across the ballroom to find Gavin. Looking into dark eyes smoldering with desire and a hint of mischief, Aimee realized how her own eyes must be glowing just like his.

Aimee grabbed both sides of his head and poured hot fire through her lips into his, whispering, "I love you, my darling."

As Gavin enfolded her in a passionate embrace, she could feel the throb of his racing heart beating in unison with her own. Buoyantly suspended in a moment of timeless wonder, they were sharing the eternal joy of truly loving, and being truly loved.

Notes from the Author

THOUGH THIS BOOK IS A NOVEL, A WORK OF FICTION, a few vignettes are based on my own personal experiences.

I would like to express my eternal gratitude to El Morya Khan, the Khan in my life and to all my beloved family and friends, as well as countless others who have inspired and supported me during the process of creating this novel of love.

And to you, dear reader, thank you for sharing in this journey.

Many Thanks!
Theresa McNicholas